MUSIC BOX MURDERS

An enthralling crime mystery full of twists

ROGER SILVERWOOD

Yorkshire Murder Mysteries Book 26

Originally published as
The Snakes and Ladders Murders

JOFFE BOOKS

Revised edition 2021
Joffe Books, London
www.joffebooks.com

First published in Great Britain in 2016 as
The Snakes and Ladders Murders

ISBN: 978-1-78931-761-9

ONE

Bluebell Wood
Two miles from Bromersley, South Yorkshire
Monday, 4 April 2016, 8.20 a.m.

Detective Inspector Michael Angel was driving the BMW passing by Bluebell Wood, when out of his eye corner he saw a naked figure with long flowing fair hair running at speed between the bushes and the trees in the same direction that he was travelling. It was a man. His chest and arms were smeared with what looked like blood.

Angel stopped the car, and rushed into the woods. But there was no sign of him. He listened a while to see if he could hear anything. He scratched his head then hung around a while, but there were no further signs. The man must have changed direction and run deeper into the woods.

Still puzzled, he returned to the car, and reached the police station in Bromersley a few minutes later. Unusually he headed straight for the control room. The duty officer was Sergeant Clifton.

'Bernie,' Angel said. 'Have you had any reports of a man missing from hospital — or anywhere else for that matter?'

'No, sir. Nothing,' Clifton said.

Angel frowned, then he told the sergeant what he had seen on his way to the station that morning.

The sergeant blinked and agreed with Angel that it was very strange indeed. Then, glancing at the occurrences book, Clifton said, 'No misper reports came in over the weekend. Apart from a domestic on Canal Road, the usual Saturday night punch up on Midland Street, and the report of an offensive smell coming from an empty block of lock-up shops, it's been an unusually quiet time.'

'Well, if there are any reports of a missing man, about forty, tall, broad shouldered, lot of fair hair, let me know.'

'Right, sir.'

Angel reached his office and began to unbutton his coat. He glanced across his desk and saw a delicious looking slice of cake on a plate along with the usual pile of letters, reports and other bumf. He blinked and wondered where the cake had come from.

The phone rang. He reached out for it.

It was Detective Superintendent Harker. He effectively ran Bromersley Police Station under the imperceptible direction of the Chief Constable.

Harker spoke breathlessly. 'Angel, I've just had a triple nine. Woman found dead.'

Angel's face muscles tightened. He pulled open the top drawer in his desk, took out a ballpoint and reached out for the top envelope from the pile of accumulated paperwork on his desk awaiting his attention. He turned the envelope over and pressed the ballpoint on it.

'The address, sir?' Angel said.

'32 Bedfordshire Gardens,' Harker said. 'Reported by Harold Kitchen who says he will stay there until police arrive. Leave it with you.'

The line went dead. The dialling tone came up. Harker had replaced the receiver. Angel tapped in a single digit.

A small female voice said, 'Cadet Jagger. Can I help you?'

He told her about the triple nine report and gave her the address.

‘Right, sir,’ she said.

Angel replaced the phone, grabbed his hat off the hook and dashed out of the office.

Although Cadet Cassandra Jagger was new to the job, the DI had trained her to carry out a routine procedure in the event of the report of an unexplained death. It was firstly to inform the Scene of Crimes Office, the pathologist, the two sergeants on Angel’s team and the inspector of the uniformed branch to supply officers to protect and guard the premises.

Angel pulled up outside the scene of the suspected murder and parked the BMW behind an old Nissan.

As he got out of the car, a man in a long light-brown warehouseman’s coat rushed down the garden path through the rose garden to the front gate.

They met on the pavement. ‘Oh Inspector Angel. You’ve been a long time,’ the man said. ‘I thought you were never coming. I’ve been on my own with her for ages. It’s not nice being on your own with a dead body.’

Angel nodded. ‘Came as soon as I could. Shall we go inside? Your name is—’

‘Harold Kitchen. Call me Harold. Follow me,’ he said.

Angel blinked. He wondered how Kitchen knew his name.

They went up the garden path, to the front of the bungalow. Angel saw that the front door had been jemmied around the lock, resulting in a splintered jamb.

Kitchen came up to him and said, ‘I broke in, you know,’ he said. ‘Mr Mitchell, the headmaster said he’d take full responsibility. It was the only way I could get into the place.’

‘It’s only a door jamb,’ Angel said.

They made their way along the hall to a door on the right to a small bedroom. In the bed was the figure of a white-haired woman with her eyes closed. She looked asleep. Angel touched her neck. It was distinctly cold and there was no pulse.

He glanced round the room. On the dressing-table was a white and gold coloured box. Could be a jewellery box. He wondered if the dead woman had been robbed. He crossed the room, took out a pen from his pocket and used it to raise the lid of the box carefully. As soon as the lid reached the ninety-degree position, a tiny doll in a tutu on a wire clicked into an upright position and rotated in various directions and speeds, seeming to dance like a ballet dancer. At the same time the tinkling of a music box played out the nursery rhyme, "Rock-a-bye baby, in the treetop." It played out the full four-line verse, rested for several seconds then repeated the action. Angel reckoned that it would have continued to repeat until the clockwork mechanism ran down. There was a tiny oval label stuck to the bottom of the end of the box. He peered down to read it. It said, "Made in China." The music box also had a small tray at the top which was removable. It had nothing in it. Suitable for rings and small brooches he thought. Using the pen and his fingernail, he removed the tray to find a space below. That was also empty. It would have been suitable for strings of pearls or a necklace. He reckoned the box could also have secreted around twenty thousand pounds in £20 pound notes or 500 grams of cocaine.

'I'll just take a look round the other rooms,' Angel said. He wanted to make sure that nobody else was still in the property. 'You can go and sit in my car, Mr er Harold, if you would like. I won't be a minute.'

Kitchen frowned then went out of the room and made for the front door.

Angel sped round the bungalow making sure that nobody was hiding in the building. Then he came out of the house and closed the door. He returned to the car as a big white van arrived. The driver, Don Taylor, the detective sergeant in charge of SOCs acknowledged Angel's wave and reversed up the drive.

Angel got into his car, turned to the man and said, 'Now then, Harold, where have you and I met before?'

'We haven't *met*, Inspector. I know you from your picture in the paper. You're the man who like the Mounties, always gets his man.'

Angel shrugged. He pointed to the bungalow and said, 'Well let's hope we get our man responsible for this, eh?' he said quickly. Then he took his small pocket recording machine from his pocket, switched it on and put it on the dashboard. 'That'll record everything we say. It'll save time if you don't object.'

Kitchen looked at it, smiled, edged closer to it and said, 'No, I don't object, Inspector.'

Angel said, 'Well, Harold, tell me who you are and how you come to find this lady dead in bed.'

Kitchen coughed to clear his throat and looking towards the recorder said, 'My name is Harold Kitchen. I am the senior caretaker at Bromersley Modern. I started work this morning at eight a.m., as usual. I switched the boilers on straightaway to get the school warm.'

'You needn't bother with your day-to-day chores, Harold. Just tell me about how you came to be at the bungalow with a jemmy in your hand.'

'Er right, Inspector,' Kitchen said. 'Miss Pierce was usually one of the first to arrive at the school. She was also one of the first to complain about things if they weren't just right. The headmaster, Mr Mitchell, arrived early and phoned me. He wanted something doing later. At about twenty-past nine, Mr Mitchell called me again. He wanted me to go to his office. When I got there, two or three other teachers were coming out looking more miserable than usual. I went in. He said that Miss Pierce had not turned up. He said he had phoned her at her home but there was no reply. All this was most strange because she was so reliable. If she had been ill or something, she would have phoned in or made contact in some way. Anyway, he wanted me to go to her house and see if she was there. None of the teachers could have gone because they all had classes to take. He himself was looking after Miss Pierce's class. So I went. It wasn't far. About four minutes in a car. I went up to the front door and rang the bell. Then I banged hard on the door using the knocker thing. Nothing. Then I peered through the letterbox. Everything looked all right. I walked round the house and looked through the windows into the rooms. In the front bedroom, I saw the form of a figure on the bed wrapped up close in bedclothes. It looked like somebody asleep. Also there was a small window at the top of the window open. I managed to open it very wide by use of a bamboo stick I took from the garden. So I shouted her name, several times, and banged hard . . . very hard on the window but I couldn't waken her up. A woman from next door came out and asked me what I was doing. I told her about it. She thought it strange. She said she didn't know Miss Pierce well, but that she seemed to be a creature of habit. We both tried again by banging and shouting. Nothing happened, so I rang Mr Mitchell on my mobile. He said she could be ill in bed and need medical attention. He suggested that should break into the house. He said he'd take full responsibility. See what the matter was, if it was life threatening, I was to deal with it, then phone him back.'

Angel nodded towards him. 'It's all right, Mr Kitchen. It's only a door. Please go on.'

'So I got a big screwdriver I have in the car,' Kitchen said, 'and prised open the front door. When we got inside, I knocked and went into the bedroom. I called out again, touched her on the shoulder and . . . well, it doesn't take a doctor to know when somebody is dead. I dialled 999, reported it to you, then I phoned Mr Mitchell. And that's about it.'

Angel nodded. 'Thank you, Harold. What was the name of the neighbour who came out to help you?'

Kitchen had to think a little while. 'Gwen, I think her name was. Mrs Cowdrey, Gwen Cowdrey. Yes, that's it.'

'And when you were in the bungalow, did you notice whether the bedroom door where you found Miss Pierce was closed or open?'

'It was closed.'

Angel smiled. 'Definitely closed,' he said. 'So our fingerprint man can expect to find your prints on the doorknob or handle?'

'I expect so, yes.'

'Do you remember what else you touched while you were in Miss Pierce's bungalow?'

'I touched her shoulder to try to wake her. I don't think I touched anything else.'

'You didn't go in any of the other rooms?'

'No. I waited by the front door. Gwen Cowdrey said I could go and wait with her in her house, but I felt responsible somehow for . . .for the place until someone took over from me.'

Angel nodded. 'Tell me, Harold, what did *you* think to Miss Pierce? Was she a nice lady? Was she a good example to the children? Was she a hard worker, do you think? Did she deserve to be a teacher of children? Was she popular? Did the kids like her?'

'I'm not sure whether the kids liked her or not, Inspector Angel. I did, because she always gave you a decision. I don't know if she was a good teacher either. She probably was. Some of those teachers don't know anything. Can't make their minds up about anything . . . always got to ask somebody else or think about it for a week or two. Miss Pierce would always say what she thought and tell you what to do without any dithering.'

Angel interpreted that to mean that she was single minded.

'Well thanks very much, Harold. If I've missed anything, I'll get back to you.'

The two men got out of the car.

Kitchen made for the Nissan car parked in front of the BMW. He started the engine and quickly pulled away from the scene.

Angel looked back to see that Dr Mac had arrived. The doctor's car was positioned immediately behind his BMW. Angel smiled approvingly. Mac was a pathologist, a Glaswegian and an old friend of his.

Then there were the cars of both of Angel's sergeants, Flora Carter and Trevor Crisp.

He made his way up the garden path to the front door of the bungalow. A uniformed PC was on duty there now also.

'Do you know where my sergeants are, lad?' he asked.

'I've seen them around somewhere, sir.'

They must have heard their names; they both showed their faces round the corner of the bungalow.

Angel said, 'What are you two playing at? Hide and seek, or doctors and nurses?'

They rushed up to him. 'We've been looking for you, sir,' Crisp said.

'We've been here about five minutes, sir,' DS Carter said.

'You didn't look very hard for me. I was in my car. I've a job for you both.'

Angel told them what he knew about the case and sent them off on the door to door, one in each direction. Then he went to the bungalow and knocked on the front door.

DS Taylor in his whites, mask and gloves opened it.

Angel said, 'Have you finished in the bedroom, Don?'

'Just about, sir,' Taylor said. 'There are no indications of foul play.'

Angel's face creased. 'What does Mac make out of it?'

'He didn't look happy, sir. Wait a moment, sir. I'll get you some gloves and you can come in and ask him yourself.'

Taylor turned away and came back in a few seconds with a little white paper bag. Angel ripped off the bag, put the gloves on and then followed the SOC man into the bedroom.

Mac also in whites was leaning over the bed. He was holding a small white gun shaped object in his hand. He saw Angel and said, 'Look here, Michael. The wonders of modern science.' He waved the instrument about. 'This is a thermometer. You stick it in any orifice of the human body and the temperature is promptly shown on the dial at the top. It's a great advance on the way we *used* to have to take the temperature of a body.' He recorded the figure onto his notepad and then put the instrument back into his bag.

Angel smiled. 'It's a change to hear you showing pleasure at something new.'

Mac blinked. 'I always give credit when it's due.'

'If you're giving credit, I'll know where to come when I'm hard up.'

Mac said, 'You'll be lucky. Neither a borrower nor a lender be. That's my motto. And you'll wanting to know at what time this poor soul died, I expect?

'It would be useful, Mac, if you have no objection. Also who killed her and how . . . would also be helpful.'

'Ever an optimist, Michael. I don't know what she died of or who was responsible. I expect to be able to tell you *what* she died of in an hour or so. *You* must find out who is responsible. I need to talk to her GP. Anybody know who it is? And I need to know if she was on any medication, prescribed or not.'

Don Taylor who had been packing a bag with specimen fingerprint cards and samples he had accumulated from the scene, said, 'We haven't found any medication of any sort yet, Doctor, but we haven't done a search in the kitchen and bathroom yet.'

'Thanks, Don,' Mac said. 'I know you will let me know if you find anything.'

Angel said, 'And I can ask that nosey parker from next door. I reckon if anyone knows who Miss Pierce's GP is, she will.'

Angel turned towards the door, then he turned back, 'Won't be a minute,' he said.

He went out through the front door and down the drive to the bungalow next door. He rang the bell and seconds later the door was opened promptly by an eager Mrs Cowdrey. Angel introduced himself and asked the question. A reply came instantly and he returned to Mac and reported the name and the practice telephone number.

'Thank you, Michael,' Mac said. 'Now the time of death would have been about three o'clock this morning . . . say between one and five a.m.'

'Right,' said Angel, writing the time on the back of an old envelope in his inside pocket. 'And you'll let me have the cause. I need to know ASAP, Mac. I'm wasting the taxpayer's money if she died from natural causes.'

The old doctor looked up. In a very quiet voice he said, 'Oh, there's one thing I'm already certain of, in this case, Michael. You're not wasting the taxpayer's money.'

TWO

Cartwright and Bowman Solicitors, Bromersley, South Yorkshire
Monday, 4 April 2016, 11.00 a.m.

The handsome Italian jumped to his feet. His face was scarlet. He glared at the solicitor at the other side of the desk and said, 'I cannot pay so much, Mr Cartwright. I am not a rich man, nor am I a poor man, but this is unreasonable. It's criminal, Mr Cartwright. It's not fair. It's not right. After all, *she* is the guilty one. In Napoli we don't have divorce it is true, but we have a fair settlement and ze wife then she go away and that . . . it is finished. But in zis case, she wants the house, a car, and half ze restaurant and money as well. *That* is unreasonable. I am a reasonable man but she is . . . a . . . a . . . a monster.'

Cartwright looked up at the young man and rubbed his chin. 'I am sorry, Mr Giannini, but in this country that is the law.'

Mario Giannini looked down at the carpet. 'Well then the law, she is a donkey. Perhaps I should not have insisted on a divorce. I should have shut my eyes and put up with her messing about with that spotty faced baboon out of ze restaurant.'

'You would not have tolerated that situation for long,' Cartwright said.

Giannini returns to his seat. 'You are right, sir,' he said. 'I would not.'

The Italian's eyes shone as they moistened at the memory of what had happened.

'When I first found out I was devastated,' he said. 'I loved her with all my heart. I felt a little guilty for spending so much time building up the restaurant, but in the long run it was for her benefit as well as my own. Nevertheless . . . I didn't know what to do, where to go. I was out of my mind. I couldn't reconcile myself to what had happened. It was difficult to face anybody . . . the staff, my customers . . . especially as I found out that the staff already knew . . . and I didn't. I was ze last to know, Mr Cartwright.'

The solicitor nodded sympathetically.

After a few moments, Giannini shrugged off the memories, sighed, looked across at Cartwright, tightened his facial muscles and said, 'Ah well, we are where we are. What's the best way out of zis mess, sir?'

* * *

Angel returned to his office in Bromersley Police Station.

The attractive slice of cake on the plate was still there looking at him. He did feel a bit hungry. He hadn't stopped all morning. He wondered where it had come from. He assumed it was for him, so he ate it and put the plate on the table behind his chair. It was delightful.

The phone rang. It was a young PC on desk duties at reception. 'There's a man here, sir, Lance White, asking to see you.'

The muscles in Angel's face tightened. He wasn't pleased. He remembered Lance White with some regret. It took him back a few years. He didn't want to see the man but he knew that he must. He had no choice.

'Get somebody to bring him down to my office, please.'

Lance White wasn't good news. Angel had made a promise to the man in exchange for Queen's evidence. The promise was made with the best will in the world. Other evidence came forward and changed the circumstances. It had all gone wrong for him and it became impossible for Angel to keep his word.

Lance White duly arrived. He was a tall, confident well set up young man in a smart suit, collar tie. He could easily be mistaken for a well to do gentleman of leisure.

Angel held out his hand to shake it. White looked at it but didn't take it.

'Sit down,' Angel said. 'You look very well.'

'I feel well . . . considering.'

'Have you got somewhere to stay?'

'Ma Johnson's doss house on Pink Street.'

Angel knew it. It was a working-man's hostel off Wakefield Road. It provided basic accommodation. Its only merit was that it was cheap.'

'When did you get out?'

'February 20. I wouldn't have thought you cared.'

'I tried to explain that the reason you got time was because your so-called friends gave evidence against you, which wasn't expected. In addition—'

'Angel, you said that if I coughed the lot, I wouldn't get more than six months. But I got *two years*. I reckon you owe me eighteen months.'

'If it had not been for Judge Sacheverell Stone, you would probably have been released with a warning. But on that day, everything that could go wrong, did go wrong, including a change in the judge. I did everything possible to get you off, both in my deposition and my evidence. Look Lance, I've explained what happened. I did my best.'

White looked at Angel severely. 'You gave me your word.'

Angel looked down. It was true. He looked up and said, 'Well, what do you want me to do about it now?'

'Huh,' White said. 'Eighteen months is a hell of a long time. You could start by offering me a fag and a glass of whisky.'

'Sorry, Lance. I don't smoke and I don't have any booze in here.'

White stretched out in the chair. 'Come off it, Michael. All high up coppers who have their own office have a bottle stashed away in a drawer somewhere.'

'Not this copper. Sorry.'

'Well, Michael, how are you going to pay me back for that eighteen months of my life?'

Angel's hands curled inwards and he bit his lip several times. He was stuck for a reply.

White said, 'Well Michael, you could offer me work for a few days, so that I can pay for my meals and bed in the hostel.'

'What work could I possibly offer you?'

'You've got a garden, haven't you? I was a gardener part of the time when I was in the Ville. Is it all up to scratch? Lawn cut, borders weeded, roses pruned, paths cleared?'

Angel wriggled uncomfortably in the chair. He did feel obliged to assist Lance White, and a full day or two in the garden by an experienced man could work wonders. In any case, Angel wasn't much interested in gardening. And it would get White from under his feet without delay. He had a desk loaded with office work needing his attention as well as a strange death to investigate.

'Very well, Lance,' he said. 'You can start today. Just for a couple of days.'

White beamed. His eyes shone excitedly. He stood up. 'I'll get off then, Michael,' he said. 'I know where you live.'

Angel stood up, reached for the phone, summoned a PC to see White off the premises.

When the door closed, Angel rubbed his chin and wondered if he would regret engaging White. He considered that he didn't really have much choice.

He promptly rang Mary, his wife and told her about the arrangement he had made with White, and that she should expect him there soon. Mary didn't sound too pleased either.

As he replaced the phone it immediately rang out again. It was Dr Mac.

'Eveline Pierce died from a snake bite, Michael,' he said. 'After the results of the blood came through, I immediately set about looking for a recent needle mark on her skin. Instead I found the tell-tale bite on her forearm.'

Angel blinked. 'A *snake* bite? She was killed by being bitten by a poisonous snake?'

'That's the size of it, Michael.'

'It wouldn't be a snake indigenous to the UK?'

'No. Probably from India or Pakistan.'

'Mmm. What can you tell me about snake bites, Mac?'

'They're painful. Not all fatal. From the shape and size of the bite it would likely be a small snake, probably about a metre long.'

'I thought snakes didn't attack humans unless they were disturbed or being attacked themselves.'

'That's generally the case, I understand.'

Angel ran his hand through his hair. 'I've got to decide whether this is a case of murder or what is laughingly called natural causes.'

'Why don't you approach the upcoming Coroner and ask him?' Mac said.

Angel shook his head. 'It would take too long. It would take two weeks to organise a Coroner's Court, meanwhile all the clues would be getting cold.'

'Well, it certainly looks fishy to me,' Mac said. 'It isn't as if poisonous snakes from India are common in Britain. This snake would have to have been stolen from a zoo or similar registered place, or smuggled into the country.'

A look of horror suddenly appeared on Angel's face. 'That snake could *still* be in Eveline Pierce's bungalow,' he said, 'in a warm place, coiled and sleeping. The SOC team should be told.'

'Aye, that's true,' Mac said.

'Better get off the line, Mac. I must warn them.'

Angel promptly phoned SOC and spoke to Don Taylor. He told them the cause of death and the dangerous possibility that the snake was still in the bungalow.

Taylor was quiet for a second then he said, 'This requires a different technique in the way that we search the place, sir.'

'I should say so,' Angel said. 'No dipping into a drawer or box of any kind with your fingers. I should tip everything out of the container onto a table or bed. And, of course, you must always wear gloves and the other protective gear.'

'I must warn the rest of the team, sir. Goodbye.'

Angel replaced the phone and it rang again.

It was DS Carter. 'I've finished the door to door, sir. Nobody has *seen* anything at all unusual. The woman next door, Mrs Gwen Cowdrey said that last night she awoke and from the direction of Miss Pierce's bungalow she thought she *heard* a tinkling sound . . . something she described as unreal . . . it was musical but she couldn't say what instrument it was . . . she only heard a few notes.'

'What time was this, Flora?'

'She said around three o'clock.'

Angel frowned. That was Mac's estimated time of Miss Pierce's death.

'What did you think to the witness?' he said. 'I've got her down as a nosey parker, but I may be wrong. Do you trust her? Do you believe her? Is she right in the head?'

'Oh I believe her, sir. I don't think she's making it up.'

He raised his eyebrows. 'Well what was the musical instrument she heard then?' he said.

'A tinkling sound, unreal . . . at the time Miss Pierce died,' Flora Carter said. 'That's weird, sir. Very weird.'

* * *

'That was very nice, Mrs Angel,' Lance White said as he noisily dropped the knife and fork on the plate.

Mary Angel looked down at the man sitting at the kitchen table. He had just finished an extra-large serving of bacon, eggs and tomatoes. He had also devoured almost half a loaf of bread.

'That's all I could think of at short notice,' she said. 'Now to follow would you like—'

'Nothing more, Mrs Angel,' he said and he patted his stomach and smiled. He looked at his watch and stood up. 'Do you want me to do the washing-up?'

Mary's eyebrows shot up. 'No thank you, Lance,' she said. 'It will only take me a minute. You'd better be off before my husband arrives.'

'Are you sure?'

The back door opened. It was Angel. He saw White. He didn't look pleased. He looked at the table and saw the dirty plate and cutlery. He glanced at Mary.

'Aye, aye,' Angel said. He had a face like thunder.

'Hello, darling,' she said.

Angel said, 'What's going on here?' He looked back at White. 'You still here, Lance? Are you on overtime?'

White took a step towards the door. 'I was just going, Michael. I'll be back in the morning, Mrs Angel,' he said. 'Nine o'clock?'

'Right, Lance,' she said. 'Thank you.'

He went out.

Angel glared at the door. When it was closed he said, 'Goodbye and good riddance.'

Mary gave Angel an angry look. 'Michael!' she said. 'He's a charming, helpful, young man.'

'He's a con man. And he's a thief, Mary.'

'Have you seen the lawn and that border at the front and the paths and the drive? It would have taken you two weekends to do all that. He's also repaired the electric kettle. He found the fault. It was the lead. He's rewired it. It works perfectly.'

'I've got to pay him for all that, you know. He hasn't done for free.'

'We can afford to be charitable to a man who has fallen on hard times, can't we?'

'Mary,' Angel said slowly. 'You shouldn't have him in the house. He's a thief. He's a liar. He'll *do* you as sure as eggs are eggs. If you want to mother him, let him eat outside in the hut or somewhere. Let him in the house and he'll be casing the joint. It's in his blood. He's doing two days' work for us to earn a bit of money, that's all.'

'He told me. And I think it is wonderful of you to be so generous towards him. As for casing the joint, what have we worth stealing?'

Angel sighed. 'Mary. That sort would steal anything. He's got me by the short and . . . I can't do anything different. He's got me in a vice.'

'What do you mean?'

He explained what had occurred two years ago and the conversation he had had with the man that morning.

Mary thought about what had transpired and said, 'Well, I would feel like he does if you had broken a similar promise made to me.'

Angel pulled a long face and sighed heavily.

'Don't forget, he is a reformed man, trying to stay respectable,' Mary said.

'Rubbish. Some do. He won't be among them.'

'He really is. The greatest thing he wants now, he told me, was a proper job, then he would settle down, be a responsible citizen, buy a house and get married.'

Angel's face muscles tightened. '*That's* the image he wants to project, Mary. All Walt Disney, sweet music and happy ever after. But you hold onto your purse and your jewellery. He'd nick that without turning a hair.'

Mary shook her head several times. 'No, Michael. You *don't* understand.'

'But I *do* understand. I understand only too well. I know these types. I've had hundreds through my hands. Handle them with care. You believe what you like love, but don't involve yourself with him in any way. Take my tip. Life is difficult enough.'

Mary wasn't convinced. She looked thoughtful and said, 'Well, Michael, I think you're wrong. But for the sake of peace and quiet, let's drop the subject.'

Angel wrinkled his nose. He wasn't happy. He unbuttoned his coat thoughtfully. He went into the hall and hung his coat on a coat hanger in the cubby hole under the stairs and returned to the kitchen.

Mary was thoughtfully washing the plate, cup and cutlery used by White.

Angel put his hands round her waist, smiled and said, 'Are we still going out then?'

She smiled, turned and said, 'I hope so. What time do we have to leave?'

* * *

Angel had reserved a quiet table for two more than a week ago at Mario's. From experience he had learned that it was necessary to book ahead if he wanted to be sure of a table.

The taxi arrived promptly at 7.15 p.m. and delivered them to Mario Giannini's restaurant about five minutes away, in the centre of Bromersley.

Mario was the handsome Italian at the entrance smiling and greeting guests as they arrived. He carried the table plan in his hand and referred to it as necessary. He showed them to their tables himself or passed them onto the pretty, petite Valerie, who charmingly delivered the guests to a table and introduced them to a waiter.

Angel's table was in a cosy cubicle near the entrance to the kitchen, the reservation desk and the cashier's kiosk. Mario had said that the food had less distance to travel so would naturally be hotter. Also we would still hear the music without being deafened by it. It was a delightful quintet who played mostly popular oldies and sometimes light classics. Angel had his back to them and faced the foyer where the entrance was and where both Mario and Valerie spent much of their time meeting and greeting.

Angel and Mary ordered the wine, the starter and the main course. They were content to sip the wine, listen to the music and — as far as Angel was concerned — watch the guests arrive.

Then the most surprising thing happened. A very smartly dressed man and woman arrived. She appeared to be laden with diamonds: on her ears, round her neck, on her wrist and on her finger.

Mario took one look at them and his hands shot up in the air in uncontrolled anger. His neck was scarlet so there was no telling how red his face was.

There was an angry exchange of words but Angel couldn't hear what was said, but obviously Mario wanted the couple to leave. Equally clearly, they intended staying. While Mario was busy arguing with the man, the woman picked up the seating plan from the waiter's desk, glanced at it, nodded, tossed it back.

Meanwhile other guests were coming in. The petite Valerie greeted them, consulted the table plan and directed them as quickly as she could away from the squabble to their tables. Then she went up to Mario and spoke to him quietly. She looked very earnest and concerned.

Mario shook his head and waved his arms like a windmill. He obviously didn't agree.

Meanwhile, the woman grabbed hold of her escort and directed him to a particular table in a cubicle directly opposite Angel and Mary. They quickly sat down.

It was clear that Mario was not pleased. It looked as if Valerie was trying to calm him down.

Angel and Mary exchanged glances.

'I wonder who they are,' Mary said.

Their waiter arrived with their starters.

Angel looked up at him and said, 'Excuse me. Do you know that couple in the cubicle directly opposite us?'

The waiter hunched his shoulders and made an unhappy face. 'That is Mr Giannini's ex-wife, Dorothy, sir,' he said. 'And that's her new partner, Adam Flagg. He used to be a waiter here.'

'Thank you,' Angel said. Then he turned to Mary. 'No wonder Mario didn't want them here.'

Then the waiter said, 'Yes, sir. And I do not think that any of the staff will serve them.'

Mary said, 'Have they been here before?'

'No, but I know that the staff support Mr Giannini,' the waiter said. 'Is there anything else?'

'No thank you.'

The waiter moved onto the next cubicle.

Angel looked round. The restaurant seemed full and the flood of arrivals had dwindled down to a trickle. Mario now met and greeted everyone himself, while Valerie could be seen behind the cashier's window already working on the preparation of the customer's bills. The quintet was playing something pastoral, there was the buzz of conversation and the noise of cutlery contacting plates.

Angel glanced across at the cubicle occupied by Dorothy Giannini and Adam Flagg. They were not eating nor drinking. There were no plates nor glasses in front of them. Angel saw Flagg accost a passing waiter who merely shook his head and walked away. Then, an angry Flagg said something to Dorothy, stormed out of the cubicle, passed behind Mario so that he didn't see him and then dashed through the waiters' IN door to the kitchen. Shortly afterwards, he returned to the restaurant through the other waiters' door with a large tray laden with covered plates, tureens, bottle of wine, glasses and appropriate cutlery. Mario was leaning down, talking to Valerie about something and missed Flagg's return, otherwise the meal would probably not have been served to a delighted Dorothy.

Shortly after that, there was a small commotion at the far end of the restaurant. A middle-aged woman was screaming and holding her throat. The man she was with stood up and asked for a doctor. The entire restaurant gazed across at the couple.

The quintet played louder to try to calm the situation.

Mario dashed down to the table and was handed a cream jug. Valerie followed him down. Mario peered into it said something and was handed a spoon. He dipped the spoon in the jug, brought it out, sniffed the cream, tasted it, and then with a flourish he put the bowl of the spoon it into his mouth and swallowed the contents. He seemed to agree it was not pleasant and he handed the jug and spoon to Valerie who passed it on to a waiter who rushed away to the kitchen with it. Mario then leaned down and briefly conversed with the couple. A moment later the well-dressed, middle-aged couple stood up, processed through the tables, past the cashier's desk displaying very disagreeable faces and out of the restaurant. Mario and Valerie followed them out.

The conversation in the room became more intense and louder. Those with a cream jug on their table looked into it. Everybody else resumed consuming the food and the drink, and listening to the music. After a few minutes everything seemed to return to normal.

Angel and Mary had finished the fish and were ready for their next course.

Their waiter duly arrived.

'Did you enjoy that, sir? Are you ready for the roast beef?'

'Yes. Thank you,' Angel said, 'What was the fuss about?'

The waiter hesitated. He looked uncomfortable. 'Somebody had deliberately put vinegar in the cream jug sir,' he said. 'But do not worry. It was only *that* jug. The cream in the churn in the cold room only delivered today is perfectly fresh and uncontaminated.'

He rushed off with the dirty plates.

Angel noticed that Mario had now taken up his position near the door looking down the restaurant. Valerie was helping out serving and clearing away dirty plates, always keeping an eye on the cashier's desk. Dorothy and Flagg were tucking into the food and drink that Flagg had earlier appropriated from the kitchen.

Suddenly a waiter with a red face rushed through the tables with a coffee pot in his hand.

Valerie saw him. She rushed into the kitchen with dirty plates.

The waiter went up to Mario and said something. Mario's lips tightened. He took the coffee pot from him, and weaved his way through the restaurant to a table for a party of six in the centre of the room. He leaned down to a gentleman who was holding a napkin to his lips. They exchanged a few words. By this time, the disturbance had caught some of the other diners' attention.

Valerie rushed from the kitchen to the scene with a coffee cup and a saucer in her hand.

Now, everybody was watching to see what the fuss was about.

Mario took the cup and poured a small amount of the liquid out of the coffee pot into it. He tried the liquid with his little finger, then swallowed the lot.

The attention of all the diners was now on Mario.

He leaned forward, looked at the gentleman and said something.

He appeared to be apologizing. The gentleman nodded. Then there seemed to be some discussion among the other five at the table.

Many diner's heads turned and whispers ensued.

Angel frowned and looked at Mary.

Eventually Mary said, 'They're saying it's gravy.'

'Gravy?' Angel said. 'Oh dear. Poor Mario.'

Mary said, 'It could have been poison.'

Angel blinked. She was right, of course.

He looked across the room at Dorothy and Flagg. He noticed that Flagg was peering round the cubicle curtain at Mario and laughingly reporting the incident to Dorothy step by step. She sat there with a glass in her hand looking unconcerned.

Angel rubbed his chin.

The discussion seemed to have become heated among the six diners on that table. A few seconds later, the man and the woman, who appeared to be his wife stood up. The four behind hesitated. They seemed reluctant to join them. There was more discussion then the four stood up, and the six unhappy souls made their way followed by Mario and Valerie out of the restaurant.

Angel said, 'Poor old Mario. It looks like six more that have had a free meal at his expense.'

Moments later, Mario and Valerie returned through the restaurant door. Mario took up his usual position trying to look composed and pleased with life. Valerie stood next to him and they conversed briefly in whispers.

Valerie saw a young couple walking towards them. The man was holding a bill. She left her position and went into the cashier's kiosk. The young man presented his bill and a credit card through the window. Valerie smiled at the man. He returned the smile, then she went through the routine concluding with giving him the receipted bill and his credit card.

'Thank you very much,' she said. 'Have a safe journey home.'

'Good night,' he said and dashed off with his wife.

Then she opened the till to put in the voucher and it was empty. It should have had a float of £300 cash in there. She closed the till and came out of the kiosk.

Meanwhile, Mario saw a table not far away where he could be helpful. A table of four had just finished their dessert and were looking round. He went over to them, took their dirty dishes away to the kitchen then came back with a basket of biscuits. He collected a cheese board from the serving table, leaned forward, lifted the cover and a mouse popped out from among the cheeses. It jumped off the board onto the table ran around it. Two women screamed. They stood up. Their napkins and some cutlery fell to the floor. The mouse then jumped off the table onto somebody's lap, onto the floor and raced across the carpet like lightening towards the kitchen. Nobody saw it after that. The two ladies stood on their chairs.

The restaurant was in uproar.

Mario's mouth dropped open. He dropped the cheese board on the table, put his hands across his stomach in dismay sighed and made his way back to his position overlooking the restaurant.

Then at the entrance to the restaurant three firemen dressed in Dayglow yellow oilskins appeared, one of them was carrying a hose.

One of them dashed up to Mario and said, 'Where is the fire, mate?'

This was about as much as Mario Giannini could take. He slumped into a chair and brought a shaky hand to his forehead. Valerie looked at him, concerned.

Another red-faced fireman said, 'We were told it was in the kitchen. How do you get there?'

Valerie stepped forward. 'Through there,' she said, pointing towards the waiters' door. 'You can also get to it outside, down the alley.'

The firemen dragged the hose through the restaurant and out by the serving door and raced into the kitchen.

Moments later, the kitchen staff in their whites, some of them dirtied with fresh soot, came into the restaurant through the waiters' door.

A tall fireman in a navy-blue uniform covered with badges and embroidered insignia appeared. He was carrying a clipboard.

Valerie came up to him.

He said, 'Where is Mr Mario Giannini?'

'I'm the manageress,' she said. 'Can I help?'

Mario heard his name mentioned. He stood up rejuvenated and said, 'I am Mario Giannini. What do you want?'

The tall fireman rushed up to him and gestured towards the diners and said, 'The place will have to be evacuated and very quickly. This is a very great risk.'

Mario shook his head then shrugged. 'Very well.'

He stood on a chair and gestured to the quintet to stop playing.

'Ladies and gentlemen,' he said. 'This has been a very eventful evening for which I apologize. The latest and final act this evening is that we have apparently a fire in the kitchen. The fire officer says to be safe we should all leave. Would you please therefore pick up your belongings and quickly leave the premises. Don't worry about the bill. Please have this evening, on me. Thank you.'

THREE

The following morning, Angel was in his office speaking on the phone to Dr Mac. He finished the call and replaced the phone.

He leaned back in the swivel chair and lightly ran his fingertips across his forehead. Mac had just confirmed that the teacher at the school had died from the bite of a snake. He rattled off the probable breed and that it was common in India and Pakistan.

How does a snake indigenous to another continent end up in a Bromersley teacher's bedroom? Angel kept coming back to this question. Or, to put it more directly: was Eveline Price's death natural or was it murder? He was reflecting on this when there was a knock at the door.

It was DS Taylor. 'Have you a minute, sir?'

'Come in, Don,' he said. 'Why, what have you got?'

'Very little, sir. There are no fingerprints, nor marks made by gloves, nor signs of any attempt to obscure prints by wiping any of the predictable places.'

Angel's mouth dropped open. 'Really?' he said. He wrinkled his nose.

Taylor nodded.

After a moment of reflection, Angel said, 'Are you saying that all the prints in the house were hers?'

'All the *recent* prints in the house were hers. There were no other clean prints.'

Angel looked into his eyes and said, 'You are sure about that, Don?'

Taylor didn't hesitate. 'Positive, sir,' he said.

Angel nodded. He accepted the point. 'I'm sure you would have said if you had found a snake or any signs of the presence of a snake in your searches.'

Taylor smiled. 'I must say,' he said. 'I find it hard to believe that she was the victim of a snake bite.'

Angel sighed. 'According to Mac, she was. And he has always been right.' Then he said, 'I suppose there is always a first time. What did you find in the vacuuming?'

'There was nothing unusual in the bag, sir. Nothing at all.'

Angel looked down at the floor then he put out the tip of his tongue and lightly licked his bottom lip thoughtfully.

Then he said, 'The bedding, Don. Any unusual marks where a snake might have been?'

'The sheets and the pillows were spotless, sir.'

'Hmmm. And the search? What did that reveal?'

'Nothing criminal, sir. I believe that she has a sister living in Preston. There was a recent letter from her. They seemed to have been on good terms. I left it where it was, on the open bureau. You'll see it.'

Angel's phone rang. He reached out for it.

It was a young PC on reception on the line. 'I'm sorry to bother you, sir. But there's a man, a foreigner by the sound of him, by the name of Mario Giannini would like to see you. He says it's urgent. Shall I tell him to make an appointment or write in?'

'Certainly not. You don't know what urgent information about some crime he might have. Did he ask for me by name?'

The PC, somewhat chastened said, 'Yes, sir.'

'For future reference, lad, if someone asks for me by name, I will always see them ASAP. Now, will you please have him escorted down to my office?'

Angel replaced the phone.

He turned to Don Taylor and said, 'Anything else?'

Taylor looked thoughtful then said, 'No, sir. There were no surprises. The victim looked just like what it says on the tin.'

Angel frowned at his answer. He didn't like these modern colloquial phrases. 'You mean she appeared to be, a respectable middle-aged, unmarried schoolteacher.'

Taylor shrugged slightly. 'Exactly, sir.'

'Right. Don. Thank you,' Angel said.

Taylor nodded and went out.

Angel tidied up his desk in readiness to receive Mario Giannini.

Moments later, a PC knocked on the door and showed the young man in. He was carrying a rolled-up newspaper.

'Ah, Inspector Angel,' Mario said. 'Please accept my sincere apologies for the disturbances and ze spoiling of your evening.'

Angel nodded and said, 'We had a lovely meal and everything for us, apart from the necessary abrupt departure, was perfect. I feel that we should pay you just the same.'

Mario held up both hands and said, 'No. No. No. Wouldn't hear of it. Several other kind people have also offered. I didn't accept *their* payment. You shall not pay either. It was a mess. It was chaos. I hope never to have to live through it again.'

Angel thought it was kind of him. He smiled and then said, 'And what can I do for you, Mario?'

'You saw what happened last night for yourself,' Mario said. 'Can you find out who is responsible and have it stopped before zay bankrupt me?'

Angel picked up the phone and summoned DS Crisp. He introduced the two men to each other then briefly brought Crisp up to date with the recent happenings at Mario's restaurant the previous evening.

Mario said, 'Fortunately nobody was hurt and ze so-called fire in the kitchen was merely a deep fat fryer on fire and out of control. It has sooted up ze kitchen. It needs re-decorating. Zat is all ze physical damages. In addition, there was the loss of takings last night amounting to several thousand pounds, and the robbery from the till of the £300 float.'

Angel looked up. 'Robbery from the till of three hundred pounds?' he said.

Mario ignored the interruption. 'I can survive all those financial losses for that *one* night, gentlemen, but no more. And the loss of reputation and clientele? Who knows? It is in *all* the newspapers. I have brought one to show you.'

It was in a small box on the front page of a national newspaper.

Angel read it carefully. 'It's been treated very lightly, Mario,' he said. 'It refers to the restaurant by name and speaks of "normally excellent food served in opulent surroundings at a down to earth price by friendly staff." You would have to shell out several thousand pounds to a top-notch public relations company to get that sort of comment in a national newspaper. It's better than paid for advertising!'

Mario's eyebrows shot up. He still wasn't pleased. 'Inspector Angel, I don't want free advertising that makes me look stupido! Look. It say something like . . . genial proprietor of ze restaurant, Mario Giannini, said he had no idea who was behind all ze tricks and stunts.'

'That's not making fun of you, Mario. It's simply saying that you don't know who is responsible. That's all.'

Mario thought a moment then said, 'But, Inspector, of course I *know* who is responsible. It's my ex-wife supported, I suppose, by that ex-waiter, Adam Flagg. She is hassling me for a divorce settlement. It is much too much.'

Angel said, 'You said something about a robbery of £300 from the cash till?'

'That is a trifling amount in zees context,' Mario said.

'Even so, tell us about it. How did it get there in the first instance?'

'It's a float, Inspector. It has been made up the day before, put in a linen bag and kept in the safe in my office. I give it to Valerie before we open each day.'

'Do you count it to see that it's correct?'

'There's no need. When Valerie cashed up, she will have counted it and selected the right number of each note and coin to make up the three hundred pounds.'

'And who checks on Valerie?'

'There's no need. I trust her implicitly.'

Angel and Crisp exchanged glances.

'You *never* check what's in the linen bag?' Angel said.

Mario raised his eyebrows and gave Angel a glassy stare. 'Inspector, there's no point in having somebody as your cashier if you don't trust them. Anyway, as things are, I trust Valerie with my life.'

Angel and Crisp exchanged glances again.

It was ten o'clock before Mario Giannini was escorted out of Angel's office to the front door by a PC from reception.

When the two policemen were alone, Angel looked at Crisp and said, 'I want you to take this case on, Trevor,' Angel said. 'Find out who is creating these nuisance incidents before Giannini goes bust. I should start by interviewing his ex-wife and her boyfriend, Adam Flagg.'

* * *

Angel stopped the BMW outside 32 Bedfordshire Gardens and made his way up the drive to the front door of the bungalow.

A PC was on duty at the front door.

'Anybody inside, Constable,' he said.

'No, sir. You're on your own,' the PC said as he turned the knob and pushed it open. 'Beware of the snake, sir,' he said with a grin.

Angel turned and looked at him. 'Why? Have you found a snake or something?'

The PC's grin grew wider. 'No, sir. But the doc says I should warn *everybody* who goes inside that there could be a snake in here, because I understand that the lady who lived here was bitten by one and she died.'

Angel pursed his lips and half closed his eyes. 'There's something I don't understand, Constable. Do you mind if I ask you a . . . an unusual personal question?'

'No, sir. Not at all.'

'Well, off the record, why did you have a grin on your face when you told me to beware of the snake?'

'Erm . . .because . . . well, sir, a poisonous snake out here? It sounds ridiculous. I mean . . . it's so unlikely that . . . a respectable mature lady schoolteacher would have a deadly poisonous snake in her bungalow in Bromersley. I mean, this isn't a jungle, or a zoo, is it?'

Angel nodded. 'No it isn't,' he said. 'I understand why you smiled, Constable. Thank you.'

He went inside the bungalow and closed the door. He was in the hall. He looked around. He went into the first room which was the front bedroom. The bed had been made and the room was very tidy. The wallpaper and paintwork looked spotless as if it had been freshly decorated. The floor was covered with a light-coloured fitted carpet that seemed to be in excellent condition. He went up to the bed Eveline Pierce had died in. He looked under the mattress. He pulled the bed away from the wall and looked down at the skirting board. He didn't know what he was looking for. He pummelled with open hands on the wall around the space the headboard covered, but there was nothing. He put the bed back to where it had been. He turned, scratched his head and looked round the room.

Among the usual dressing-table accoutrements he saw the white and gold coloured music box. It seemed out of keeping with the rest of the house contents. He remembered. It played a delightful tune, enjoyable the first time you hear it but screamingly awful after it has been played several times and more.

He saw the window. He had previously observed that the top window had been left in the open position the night the woman had died. So it was reasonable to assume that entry by a snake, if it had been so motivated, would not have been difficult. Who would know what motivated snakes? Food, sex, companionship or shelter, he thought. In this situation, all that Eveline Pierce had to offer was shelter in the form of a comfortable, warm bed. Heat might be important to a hot-blooded snake used to 40 degree temperatures in India or Pakistan. It could have insinuated its way under the duvet, discovered a spot where it could enjoy the body heat transmitted by Eveline Pierce, rolled itself into a coil and dropped off to sleep until it was disturbed. What motivated it to bite the lady and then disappear he had no idea. And where was the snake at that time?

Angel had a quick meander round the other rooms, decided that he wasn't really learning anything there anymore. He came out of the house, nodded at the PC on the door and made his way down the drive to his car. Then he heard somebody calling. It was a woman's voice.

'Inspector Angel! Inspector Angel!'

He turned round to see Eveline Pierce's next-door neighbour, Gwen Cowdrey, half out of her bungalow's front room window.

He stopped and said, 'Oh? Good morning, Mrs Cowdrey. What can I do for you?'

'Wait right there, Inspector, *please*,' she said. She closed the window and seconds later appeared at her front door. She came down the drive. He went up to meet her.

'I wanted to ask how you are getting along with the case, Inspector?' she said.

She was all mouth and spectacles.

'I know I shouldn't ask things like that,' she said, 'but I did so like Miss Pierce and as a long-time neighbour of hers and saw and spoke to her almost every day, you will naturally understand that I am concerned.'

Of course he understood. He wondered what to say. He decided on the very brief truth. 'It's early days yet, Mrs

Cowdrey. We are following up several lines of inquiry. That's all I can say.'

'Have you found the snake? I don't mind telling you, Inspector, I was not pleased to hear that Miss Pierce was in her own bed minding her own business when she was bitten and then died, just like that! The thing is, have you found that wretched snake?'

'No we haven't. It is awful, I know,' Angel said.

'Inspector Angel, I live here on my own and I am not usually afraid of anything, but to think that a poisonous snake that had killed my friend next door, could still be around and could slither into my bedroom, keeps me awake.'

'I'm sure that that snake, if it was a snake, will be miles away by—'

Mrs Cowdrey's eyes flashed. 'What do you mean *if* it was a snake?'

Angel bit his lip. His tongue had been ahead of his subconscious mind. He had been toying with the possibility that the snake bite marks on Evelyn Pierce's arm were faked by a specially made tool and that they had been inflicted moments after the murderer had injected by a hypodermic syringe a fatal dose of snake venom while the poor woman slept. However he had not thought the idea through completely. There may be no grounds to follow that idea at all. There might very well be a live snake.

'A slip of the tongue, Mrs Cowdrey, I assure you. It *was* a snake . . . I was saying that it could now be miles away by now.'

She didn't look convinced. 'And what about the tinkling music I heard the night she died?'

'I thought you said you only "*thought* you heard a tinkling sound of a few notes"?'

'I did, but the more I think about it the more convinced I am that in fact I did hear it.'

Angel's eyes half closed. His hand went to his chin. Eventually he said, 'I would like to try an experiment. Will you assist me?'

Mrs Cowdrey smiled, wriggled her shoulders and said, 'An experiment, Inspector? On me?'

Angel said, 'The tinkling sound you told my sergeant you thought you heard early yesterday morning . . . where were you exactly when you heard it?'

'I was in bed. I had woken up. I don't know why.'

'I want to reproduce the conditions exactly as they were that night. Will you go back to your bungalow, close or open the doors and windows to position them as they were on Sunday night early Monday morning, then lie on the bed and listen up?'

She rushed off. There was a lightness in her step. She was pleased to be the centre of an experiment.

Angel tried to see if Mrs Cowdrey could hear the music box from inside Miss Pierce's bedroom and she could not. He found that very strange. He tried the bathroom, the kitchen and the hall also with negative success. He stood outside the front door with the police constable looking on mystified at what was happening. Angel raised the lid of the music box briefly; it played several notes. Then he waited for a report from her.

Moments later Mrs Cowdrey came running out of her bungalow, smiling widely. 'That's it, Inspector. That's what it sounded like.'

'Thank you very much, Mrs Cowdrey,' he said and then he went into the bungalow and closed the door. He stood in the hall and scratched his head. Mrs Cowdrey *couldn't* hear the music box when played in the bedroom. She *could* hear it when he was stood at the front door. But why on earth would the murderer stand at the front door and play it? Why would he play the music box at all?

Angel was both pleased and sad. He was pleased that he had discovered the possible place where the music box had been played, but sad because, as snakes could not open and close music boxes to order, it showed that the death was no accident, but that a human must have been involved and therefore that Miss Pierce had been murdered.

FOUR

Angel parked the BMW among the dozen other cars outside Bromersley Modern School. It was half past twelve, lunch break, and the pupils were in the playground shouting, screaming and running after a ball, or leaning against the railings reading or fiddling with their mobile phones.

Angel weaved his way through them, went inside the building, found the secretary's office, introduced himself, discovered that her name was Helen Thickett, showed his ID, then said, 'I'm looking into the death of Miss Eveline Pierce. What can you tell me about her?'

Helen Thickett blinked and said, 'Well, what do you want to know, Inspector? I mean, there's such a lot to say. She'd been here many years. She had been here longer than anybody else. I can tell you that she taught geography.'

'Would you say she was a popular teacher?'

Helen Thickett hesitated, then she said, 'I believe that she was the best disciplinarian in the school. She will be missed.'

Angel raised his nose, lowered it and said, 'Yes, but was she a popular teacher?'

'Inspector, I don't believe you should speak ill of the dead.'

Angel pursed his lips. 'Oh I see. You think that we should not try to find out the truth, if it requires someone to say something unkind or critical of the victim. You believe that if someone is murdered, we should not make a sensible attempt to discover the identity of the murderer to prevent him or her doing it again?'

'Murdered? Oh. I didn't mean that, Inspector. I mean . . . I didn't know that Miss Pierce had been *murdered*.'

Angel nodded lightly.

Helen Thickett said, 'Well, I think you should see our head teacher, Mr Mitchell, Inspector, and address that question to him.'

Angel's lips tightened. 'What's the matter, Miss Thickett? Do you not have a mind of your own? I *will* be seeing your head teacher, Mr Mitchell, and I may very well be asking him what he thought of Miss Pierce, but I will most definitely not be asking *him* what *you* thought of her.'

Helen Thickett sighed. 'Well, all right, if you must know, she wasn't very nice. She used to come in here pepper me with questions about all sorts of things to do with the pupils or the school. And when I didn't have the immediate answer on the tip of my tongue, she used to sniff and walk out. I could have found out the answers to her questions if she had given me time, but she never did. And she didn't ever ask if she could see Mr Mitchell. If she wanted to see him, she used to walk past me and go straight into his office. He may have had parents in there, a school governor or even an examiner; many a time, he wasn't in there at all. When I asked her to check with me to see Mr Mitchell, before bursting in on him — after all, that's partly what I was there for — she said that when she started teaching there wasn't such thing as a school secretary . . . making my job seem unnecessary. She was awful.'

Angel nodded. 'And do you know why she was rude to you?'

'No. She was just that way out. She doesn't like anybody really.'

'How did she get along with the children then?'

'They were terrified of her. Most of them.'

Angel shook his head.

There was a knock on the door behind him.

The door opened and a man's head popped through. It had a lot of silvery white hair, a white moustache, a tanned skin and a ready smile. The man looked at Angel and then at Helen Thickett.

She stood up. She became another woman. Her face brightened. She smiled and said, 'Mr Glover. Do come in.'

'Good morning, Helen,' Glover said. 'Am I intruding?'

She introduced the two men to each other and they shook hands.

Angel noticed that she hardly ever took her eyes off the silvery white-haired man, who he discovered was Gordon Glover, chairman of the board of governors of the school.

Glover immediately looked at Angel and said, 'I actually came to see the senior master, Leslie Mitchell about Miss Pierce, Inspector. It's a bit of a shock. May I ask if that is what has brought you here?'

'Yes, indeed,' Angel said.

Glover frowned. His eyes made small movements to the left, then to the right and then back again finally coming to rest. 'Did she not die a natural death? A heart attack or something like that?'

Angel gave him the minimum information to which Glover responded with raised silver eyebrows and a slow shaking of the head. 'Murder,' he said.

Then Angel said, 'Was she a popular teacher?'

'She'll be sadly missed,' Glover said.

'But *was she popular*?' Angel said.

'She always produced the best examination results, on average,' Glover said.

Angel and Glover stared at each other.

Then Glover said, 'Well, if you insist, Inspector. I wasn't her greatest fan, but she was a damned good teacher. She got results which some teachers hadn't a cat in hell's chance of getting or bettering. The school is going to have difficulty replacing her, especially midterm.'

Angel said, 'Do you know of any reason why anybody would want her dead?'

'Certainly not,' Glover said. 'Ridiculous idea.'

Angel looked at the secretary.

She looked from Glover to Angel and said, 'Erm . . . no. Absolutely not.'

The door suddenly opened behind them. A man came in carrying a load of paper files under his arm.

Helen Thickett stood up. 'Ah. Mr Mitchell.'

Mitchell glanced from Glover to Angel and frowned.

Helen Thickett introduced Angel to Mitchell.

'The police?' Mitchell said. 'Are we in trouble, Inspector?'

'I shouldn't think so, Mr Mitchell. I have to ask you a few questions about Miss Eveline Pierce,' Angel said. 'Won't take long.'

Glover looked at Mitchell and said, 'Sorry to hear the news, Leslie. We need to act promptly. I have to talk to you very soon. I see you are busy. I've another call to make. I'll come back in half an hour.'

Mitchell said, 'Right, Gordon.'

'Nice to have met you, Inspector,' Glover said and he hurried out of the small office.

As he was closing the door, Angel noticed that Glover and Helen Thickett exchanged the slightest of glances.

Mitchell made for the door to his office which was at the side of Helen Thickett's desk. He turned to Angel and said, 'You'd better come through into my office, Inspector. We can speak in private. Please sit down. Hope you haven't been waiting long.'

Angel pulled up a chair and sat down.

'It's been a perfectly dreadful morning,' he said. He puffed out a lungful of air as he unloaded the files he was carrying onto his desk. 'As Miss Pierce is no longer with us, somebody has to keep her classes quiet and controlled, and we simply haven't the staff. Now then, Inspector what do want to see me about?'

Angel told him that the police believed that Miss Pierce had been murdered. Mitchell expressed sadness and surprise.

Angel said, 'Did you know of anyone who would want her dead?'

'Certainly not,' Mitchell said. She may not have been a popular teacher, but I am not aware of anybody who would have wished her dead. She crossed the paths of many young types educated out of their class, in appointments senior to hers, who couldn't agree on the time of day, but that was a long way from wishing her dead.'

Angel nodded. 'Did Miss Pierce have any kind of social life?'

'Not that I know about. What teachers do out of school is up to them of course, I don't pry, Inspector.'

The phone rang. Mitchell picked it up. It was Helen Thickett from the outer office.

'Sorry to interrupt, Mr Mitchell, but it's Mr Khan again,' she said. 'Could you possibly see him? He's worried about Sahil. I noticed he was marked absent again on the register this morning.'

Mitchell hesitated. He turned to Angel. 'Is it possible . . . would you mind, Inspector? It's a bit of an emergency . . . if I saw a parent, who is upset about his son who has bunked off school again? He is very worried. It should only take five minutes or so. You can stay.'

Angel could hardly say no. He smiled and nodded. 'Of course.' He stood up. 'Where can I go?'

'No,' Mitchell said. 'There's no need for that. Please sit down. You may be needed anyway.'

Into the phone Mitchell said, 'Send Mr Khan in, Helen.' Then he replaced the phone in its cradle.

A small, well-dressed man wearing a white turban came into the office. He started speaking as soon as he opened the door. 'O dear me, Mr Mitchell sir, I am out of my mind with worry. Sahil left home this morning after prayers at twenty minutes to nine o'clock. I thought he was coming straight to school. He told me that he would do that, but clearly, he has not told me the truth. He has taken with him his mobile phone, but when I ring him, he does not answer. I am very worried. I do not know where he can be.'

Khan suddenly noticed Angel. He stared at him. He didn't look pleased. He peered at Angel and then said, 'Peace be with you, sir.'

Angel indicated the chair nearest to him. 'Thank you, Mr Khan, and peace be with you also.'

Khan sat down.

Mitchell said, 'This is Inspector Angel of Bromersley Police. You don't mind if he stays, do you?'

Khan jumped up. There was panic on his face. 'I don't need the police, Mr Mitchell, sir. Leave the police out of this. This is dreadful. O dear me. The police cannot help me . . . this is a family problem . . . not a police matter.'

'Have no fear, Mr Khan,' Mitchell said. 'The police are only interested in crime. If there is no crime, the police are not the slightest bit interested.' He looked at Angel and said, 'That's true, isn't it, Inspector?'

Angel nodded. 'Absolutely. Believe me, Mr Khan, we have far too much serious crime on our files. Our time is fully committed. However, that doesn't preclude me from assisting in the *prevention* of crime.'

Khan shook his head and said, 'O dear me. I hope so. Thank you Inspector, sir.' He resumed his seat.

Mitchell said, 'Did you find out why he did not check in to school the last time?'

'He simply does not like school, Mr Mitchell, sir.'

'That seems unlikely, Mr Khan. He is good at sports. I've seen him on the field. It's an absolute delight to see him score a goal for the school team and he enjoys it too. You can see it on his face. Also I remember he positively shines in 10Q at history, mathematics and chemistry, where he is always awarded As.'

Khan shrugged. 'Well that's what he tells me anyway, Mr Mitchell, sir. He simply does not like school.'

'And do you know *where* Sahil went on the other occasions he played truant?'

Khan looked down and said, 'No. And he would not tell me where he had been. So I think that it must be some place I have forbidden. I have thought long about this. He must have gone . . . o dear me . . . to my late wife's sister's house. That is a shameful house. A disgraceful house. God will punish them for their iniquity.'

Mitchell said, 'Why is your late wife's sister's house disgraceful and shameful?'

'O dear me,' Khan said. 'It is too painful for me to say.'

Mitchell wondered what to reply. He and Angel exchanged glances.

Then suddenly Khan said, 'They have three daughters and only *one* is betrothed! . . . There, I have said it. May God forgive me.'

Mitchell frowned. 'I don't understand,' he said.

Khan said, 'They have two daughters *not* betrothed, aged sixteen and nineteen years. They are well passed puberty. My son, Sahil, was betrothed before he was ten. He is now almost sixteen.'

'To one of them?'

'Oh no no. To a girl from a very good wealthy family back home. Her father is a jeweller.'

Mitchell said, 'Mr Khan, I still do not understand why you say your late wife's sister's house is disgraceful.'

'How can I explain. It is custom in our tradition to have all your children — particularly if they are girls — betrothed before they reach puberty. If your child is not betrothed, it suggests that — in other people's eyes — your child is ugly, and if your child is a girl, that you are too poor to provide her with a good dowry. My sister-in-law and her husband should have had both their daughters betrothed by now. They are beautiful girls and their father is very wealthy.'

'So both daughters seem adequately qualified for betrothal, so what is wrong with your son visiting his aunt and uncle's house?' Mitchell said.

Khan's jaw muscles tightened. He uncrossed and re-crossed his legs. 'Oh dear me. I thought I had explained all that, Mr Mitchell, sir. He might find or have found an interest in one or other of the daughters.'

Angel said, 'Do you mind me saying something?' He looked at Khan and said, 'Well, why don't you go round there and find out?'

Khan's face dropped. 'Oh dear me. I can't be seen going *there*, Inspector, sir.'

'Well, you could phone them?' Angel said.

Khan blinked.

Angel said, 'Nobody would know that you've phoned. If he *is* there, it would settle your mind, wouldn't it? And you can decide what to do after you have spoken to him.'

Khan smiled. 'It would, sir. I can.' He sighed heavily.

Mitchell said, 'You can use the phone in the outer office. Tell Miss Thickett I said it was all right for you to make a call.'

Khan stood up. He turned to Mitchell and then Angel in turn and said, 'Thank you. Peace be with you, kind sir.'

Mitchell said, 'Thank you, Mr Khan. I hope the phone call is fruitful.'

'And peace be with you,' Angel said.

Khan turned and made for the door.

* * *

It was four o'clock before Angel arrived back in the office. And there was another slice of cake on a plate on his desk.

He frowned as he unbuttoned his coat, took off his coat and hung it up.

He reached out for the phone and tapped in a number.

A young voice answered, 'Cadet Jagger, sir.'

'Any messages, Cassie?'

'Yes, sir. DS Crisp asked where you were. I told him. He said he'd see you later. And your wife phoned. She said it wasn't urgent, but would you ring her before you leave the office. That's all, sir.'

'Right,' he said. 'Thank you. Oh, Cassie, I've found a piece of delicious looking cake on my desk . . .'

'It's for you, sir. To have with your tea. It's orange cake. Fresh out of the oven this morning. Bought it from that bakers on the corner of Church Street. The Paradise cake shop.'

'You shouldn't have, Cassie. Well, thank you.'

He held onto the handset, pressed down the cradle to cancel the call, scrolled down to his home number and clicked on it. As it rang out, he reached out to the plate, broke a piece of the slice of cake off and put it in his mouth. It didn't take any chewing. It dissolved delivering a sweet orangey taste.

Mary answered the phone.

'Oh, Michael, I'm glad you rang. Lance has been here all day. He's almost finished weeding the garden. He's clipped all the hedges, cut the lawn, strimmed round and mended the light outside the front door. It hasn't worked for ages. You won't have to do anything in the garden for ages. I am so pleased, Michael, that I've given him the alarm clock from the side of our bed. He has so little and he was hinting that that was one thing he really needed. And it is quite old. We must have had it ten years or more. I hope you don't mind.'

Angel sighed. He certainly *did* mind. 'Well, what am I going to use to waken me up for work?'

'We can get another. They don't cost the earth. I thought I should let you know so that you could call in at Jeeves on Market Street and get one.'

'*Jeeves*! That's a jeweller. The most expensive shop in town. I'll enquire at that new pound shop.'

'You'll not get one from a pound shop!'

'Well, I'll see,' he said wrinkling his nose. 'It's going to be a damned costly day; I can see that. I have to *pay* him today as well.'

'Yes, love, but look what you've saved. By the way, all day, the lights have been flickering and there has been a lot of interference on the radio as if the electricity supply was being interrupted.'

Angel groaned. 'Anymore news to cheer me up?'

'Well, I have to tell you . . .or . . .or what else would I do?'

'Of course you do, love. Don't worry about it, Mary. I'll try and be a bit early and sort it out.'

He finished the call and put the phone back in its cradle. He didn't like it. He didn't like it one bit, but Mary wasn't exaggerating. He had noticed the light in the bathroom flickering early that morning. He *might* be put to the expense of an electrician. He didn't want that.

He saw the remainder of the slice of cake on the plate. He reached out for it and finished it off.

There was a knock at the door. It was DS Crisp.

'Come in, lad. What did you want?'

'This Mario Giannini robbery case I am on, sir . . .'

'Yes, Trevor. Sit down. What about it.'

Crisp sat down, took out his notebook, turned back a few pages and said, 'I have seen the CCTV and it looks as if the only people who were *seen* anywhere near the cash kiosk since the float money was put in the till were Valerie Downing, Mario Giannini, and a waiter called Stefan Peruzzi.'

Angel nodded and said, 'Go on.'

'So I interviewed him. He fervently told me he had *not* taken the money. He said that he would rather cut off his right arm than steal from Mario Giannini. He claimed that he had a long-term friendship with Mario.'

'I asked both Valerie Downing, and Mario Giannini, separately, what they knew about Stefan Peruzzi. Mr Giannini said that out of all the staff at Mario's, Stefan was the most unlikely thief among them. Mr Giannini said that Stefan had worked for him from the very first day he had opened a little café in Cudworth in 1999. And Miss Downing said that he was the most honest and straight man there. I checked with Records and Stefan Peruzzi is not known to us, neither are Valerie Downing and Mario Giannini.'

'Did you interview Mario's ex-wife and the man with her, Adam Flagg?'

'Yes, sir, of course. They were both outraged that I should be asking them questions that suggested that they could possibly be guilty of stealing anything. And they both had nothing but nasty comments to make about Mario Giannini and Valerie Downing. There are no witnesses or forensic, so I couldn't take it any further.'

The corners of Angel's mouth turned down. 'That's a very strange phenomenon about human nature,' Angel said. 'One can change from earnest passionate love for somebody to merciless fanatical hate in a very short time.'

Crisp blinked.

Angel suddenly sat up in the chair, looked at Crisp and said, ' Well lad, what are you going to do now?'

Crisp's eyes widened. His mouth dropped open. 'Erm. I don't think there's anything more I can do, sir.'

Angel suddenly glared at him. 'Are you going to leave the case at that then?' he said. 'Case closed?'

Crisp didn't know what to say. If he said yes, Angel would bawl him out. If he said no, Angel would ask him what lines of inquiry he was to follow and he didn't have any.

'Erm. I'm still thinking about it.'

Angel's lips tightened back against his teeth. 'Well I'll think about it for you,' he said. 'There were various disturbances made during the evening. There was the finding of the curdled cream. You could try and find out who prepared the cream? How many hands it had passed through before it arrived at the table. Where was the vinegar kept? Fingerprints on the bottle? How was it possible that the two items came together and nobody saw it? Then there was the mix up of the gravy with the coffee. A coffee pot is quite distinctive and the pouring of coffee into a gravy boat should, one would have thought, be seen by somebody. Then there's the mouse on the cheeseboard. Where did the mouse come from? Anybody known to breed or keep mice? And so on. There's enough there to keep you going for a couple of days, so *crack on with it*!'

FIVE

It was five a.m., early Wednesday morning, 6 April. It was as dark as a burglar's blackjack. No traffic hum, no owls hooting, no birds tweeting, not even a fly buzzing at the window bottom disturbed the golden silence. Most of the respectable world were at peace, resting, restoring themselves for the next day's battle for a better life.

Michael and Mary Angel, tangled in each other's arms, were sleeping the sleep of the good, oblivious to the world.

The telephone rang.

Michael Angel rolled away from his wife and stared out into the darkness.

The bell was raucous and insistent.

Angel reached out in the darkness. Eventually he located it and put it to his ear. 'Yeah?'

'Who is that?' a young voice demanded.

'The Bishop of Durham,' Angel growled. 'Who is that?'

'Oh, sorry to disturb you, sir,' the voice continued. 'This is DS Merriman, duty officer, Bromersley Police. Can I speak to DI Angel please?'

Angel yawned then said, 'Speaking Merriman, what's up?'

'We've had a triple nine, sir. Woman reported hearing unusual noises of an intruder in the night, subsequently she found her lodger dead.'

'What time is it?'

'Five past five, sir.'

'Right. I'll come straightaway. Will you inform DS Taylor, Dr Mac and DS Carter, please? And what's the address?'

* * *

Forty-two minutes later, Angel stopped the car at 8 Beechfield Walk, Bromersley. It wasn't difficult to find. Amidst an elegant estate of detached houses built in the early 1900s, it was the only building with lights on.

Angel leaped out of the car, through the gate, up the path to the front door. It opened before he found the bell push.

A pale faced woman in her sixties said, 'Are you the police?' Her bottom lip trembled. 'It's awful. Really awful.'

Angel nodded. 'Take it easy, now, love. Where's the victim?'

'Follow me, he's upstairs.'

He followed her through the hall up the staircase, along the landing and through a door to a large room bulging with furniture. At the far end was a bed. He could see the head and shoulders and the outline of a figure of somebody — a man.

Angel went straight up to the figure. There were no obvious signs of injuries, no signs of any blood.

Angel put his fingers on the neck. The body was still warm, but there was no sign of a pulse.

He turned to the woman and said, 'Did you call a doctor?'

She looked at Angel affronted. She breathed loudly through her nose. 'I know when somebody's dead, Inspector. I was a nurse for eighteen years.'

Angel didn't think that either of them were qualified strictly speaking to pronounce that a man was dead. But, to be reasonable, the man certainly looked very dead and definitely beyond revival. The body was that of an overweight man who had a red podgy face. He looked about fifty years of age.

Angel looked round the room. There was a lot of furniture for its size. It had a bed and a wardrobe at one end, and a writing desk, a table, an easy chair, a bookcase and a TV at the other. The components of a model bedsit, he thought.

'Can we go somewhere and talk?' he said.

She directed him downstairs.

'You didn't touch anything or move anything after you found the man dead, did you,' he asked as they reached the hall.

She breathed loudly through her nose again. 'I'm not altogether an idiot, Constable,' she said. 'I watch a lot of films on TV. I know what goes on in cases of murder.'

He hid the wry smile and said, 'I have to ask. It's extremely important to our forensic team.'

The doorbell rang. They both went to answer it. It was Don Taylor and his team of three already togged out in the white suits, hoods, wellingtons and masks and carrying large white canvas packs filled with cameras, lights, vacuums and sample containers.

Angel said, 'Now, Don, one victim. Male. First floor. Turn left at head of stairs, second door on the right.'

'Right, sir,' Taylor said and the team made for the stairs.

Angel went to close the front door when he saw DS Carter's face appear out of the dark.

'Sorry I have been so long, sir,' she said.

'Come in, Flora,' he said. 'There's a murdered man upstairs. But he hasn't been dead long. See if you can see anybody around in a vehicle or on foot who seems suspicious. Or investigate any house nearby with a light on. Ask if they heard anything in the last three hours or so. It's a long shot, but see what you can do.'

'Right, sir,' she said and she went out.

Angel closed the front door and turned back to the lady of the house. 'Will they be wanting any teas or coffees?'

'No thank you. At least, not until they've finished all they have to do. That would be in six or eight hours or more.'

She nodded moved down the hall, opened a door, switched on the light and said, 'Will this be suitable?'

It was a small comfortable-looking sitting room.

'Ideal,' he said. He went in and sat down in an easy chair facing a coffee table. 'May I sit here?' he said.

She selected a similar chair and sat opposite him.

Angel took the small personal pocket tape recorder out of his pocket and put it on the table in front of them. 'Do you mind if I record what we say? It will save time taking notes.'

He switched it on. A little red light showed it was recording.

'What is your name, please?'

'Elaine Lax, Mrs,' she said.

He told her his name then he said, 'Who lives in this house besides you and your husband?'

'My husband left me a long time ago, Inspector. He left me with a thumping great mortgage on this house. I have no idea where he is or what happened to him. John Logan *was* my lodger. He is the man upstairs who is . . . dead.' She quickly reached into a pocket in the dress and found a screwed-up tissue. She wiped a tear from an eye. 'Mr Logan has been my lodger, a model lodger, if the truth be told, for twelve years. As I have been a model landlady, I hope.'

'And Mr Logan was in work?'

'He was a teacher at Bromersley Modern. He taught Latin.'

Angel's mouth dropped open. His heart seemed to stop momentarily then pound hard rapidly.

Elaine Lax noticed the change in him. 'What's the matter, Inspector?'

'I was just thinking,' he said. 'Tell me exactly what happened then?'

'A very strange thing. John had a music box delivered in the post yesterday.'

Another bell rang in Angel's mind. 'A music box?' he said slowly and deliberately.

She peered at him and frowned. 'Yes, a cream and gold coloured thing. Whatever's the matter?'

He jumped up, leaned over the coffee table and pressed the hold button on the tape machine. 'Excuse me for a moment, Mrs Lax,' he said. 'There's something I must do. Won't take a second.'

He went out of the hall, mounted the stairs three at a time, went up to John Logan's bedsit, where his dead body was, and where SOC were working. He tapped on the door. It was opened by Don Taylor.

Angel pointed beyond the man and said, significantly, 'I have just discovered that the victim was a teacher at Bromersley Modern, so you need to be *very* careful.'

Taylor's jaw dropped. 'You mean there might be a snake running around loose?' he said.

Angel nodded. 'Possibly. Be very careful. Have you had a good look at the dead man yet?'

'No, sir. We've vacuumed him and his bedspace, sir, but the rest is in Dr Mac's regimen. Has he been told, by the way?'

'Should have been. I don't expect he'll be long. By the way, I need two pairs of gloves for the witness and me?'

'Yes, sir,' Taylor said and turned to address his team. 'DI Angel says that there is the possibility of a poisonous snake in the house, so be very wary.'

There were murmurs of horror and disgruntlement.

Angel understood their fears and he massaged his lower lip between his teeth.

Taylor returned with two white packets of rubber throw-away gloves.

'Good luck, Don,' Angel said. Then he took the packets and dashed down one flight back to the ground floor to the sitting room.

'Sorry about that,' he said as he bustled in. He gave a pair of gloves to the witness. 'Put those on, Mrs Lax, and don't take them off. I'll tell you why.'

He told her about the murder of Eveline Pierce and explained why she needed to wear the gloves and take precautions against the possible presence of a poisonous snake in the house.

Her eyes flashed. 'Oh no. I couldn't bear that,' she said as she shuddered.

Angel said, 'If it is any comfort, Mrs Lax, we didn't find a snake in Miss Pierce's bungalow and it was thoroughly searched.'

'I don't like snakes,' she said, 'slithering about the place.' Her whole body trembled.

'No, well I don't suppose it's here now,' he said trying to appease her. 'Now you were telling me that Mr Logan received a music box. Did he say who it was from?'

'He didn't know who it was from, Inspector. Very strange that, I thought.'

'And erm . . . what did Mr Logan think to it?'

She hesitated then said, 'Well, he played it a few times. I think he liked it. I found it very annoying. Anyway, his bed on the first floor is directly under mine. And he was playing it in the night and it woke me up. He played it over and over. It only plays one tune.'

'And what is it? Do you know?'

'Of course I know. It has nearly sent me daffy. It's rock-a-bye baby on the treetop.'

Angel nodded. 'I thought it would be,' he said. 'What time was this?'

'It was exactly four o' clock when it started. I didn't bother at first. But it persisted. I decided to go down to ask him to stop. I switched on my light, put on my dressing gown and went down. By the time I got there, of course, as is always the case, it had stopped. Anyway I knocked on the door and called out. I waited a little, knocked again there was still no reply, so I went in. The room was in darkness. I couldn't see anything, so I spoke to him so that he wouldn't be startled. I put the light on and saw him in bed, just as he was when you saw him. I tried for a pulse but there was no sign of life. And then I broke down. I think I must have had a soft spot for him somewhere. He was always very straight with me, as I was with him. But our worlds were miles apart. Of, course he was an educated man, taught Latin and was fluent in Greek, French, German and English, of course. My subjects were more mundane, washing-up and managing my domestic requirements on a small, fixed income. Anyway, I said a little prayer for his soul. I suppose you think that was daft?'

'Not at all.'

They looked at each other, smiled, then after a quiet moment Angel said, 'And then what did you do?'

'Well, I came downstairs here and dialled 999.'

'Did you happen to notice where the music box was? Was it in his hands, on the bed, the bedside table or where?'

'I didn't see it. I forgot all about it.'

'Do you know how he came by it?'

'It came in the post yesterday morning, I remember. It was a bit unusual. John rarely received parcels, and when he did it was usually a book.'

'Have you still got the wrapping?'

She blinked several times. Then jumped up. 'It'll be in the waste bin in the kitchen. I empty his waste basket into there every day.'

She dashed out to the kitchen. Angel followed. With Don Taylor's help, they managed to salvage the brown paper wrapping and the plastic bubble wrap the music box came in.

* * *

Two hours later, after Angel had consumed two bacon sandwiches and a mug of coffee kindly prepared and served by Mrs Lax in her kitchen, he was advised by a constable sent down by Sergeant Taylor from the SOC team that they had finished at the scene of the crime.

Angel quickly put the rubber gloves back on, climbed the stairs and went into John Logan's room.

Dr Mac who was busy packing up his bag at the side of the bed, looked up at him.

Angel was making his way across to DS Taylor, who was busy with one of his team flashing a camera around the bed and the dead man on it, when his attention was drawn to what he saw on the top of the desk. It was a music box. It looked exactly the same as the one he had seen at Eveline Pierce's bungalow. He could see it was covered in aluminium powder so it had been checked for prints. He picked it up, lifted the lid and the mechanism began. It was the same "Rock-a-bye baby" tune. He closed it, replaced it, frowned and rubbed his chin.

Taylor went across to him.

Angel looked up. 'Well, Don, what have you got?' he said.

'Very little, sir. Of course it's the same MO. No recent fingerprints or footprints. Like the Pierce case, it looks as if nobody came into the room.'

'Was the window open?'

'Only the top one, sir,' Taylor said.

Mac leaned forward and said, 'I'll tell you what happened, Michael. A snake came into the room, climbed up the leg of the bed, traversed its way along the duvet to the sleeper's neck, bit the poor man and then—'

Angel said, 'Opened the lid of the music box for a little while, played a few verses of "Rock-a-bye baby," then closed it, put the music box under its arm, caught a passing pigeon who flew it from the bed across the room to the desk, where it placed the music box in the middle of the desk, then the pigeon and the snake disappeared in a puff of smoke.'

Taylor smiled.

Mac turned and looked at Angel and said, 'Tha's no need for the sarcasm, Michael.'

'Well, if the only human in the room was the dead man, who played the music box *after* the snake had bitten him?'

Mac busied himself packing his bag and avoided Angel's eyes.

Angel said, 'What's the matter, Mac, the cat got your tongue?'

'I'm not here to answer your puzzles, Michael. I am here to furnish you with facts supported by science, when I can.'

'All right, Mac, we are being serious now, are we? Well what have you got so far?'

'Well, this man died between three and four a.m. of a snake bite. He does not appear to have any other injury, but I will give you a full report when I have done the post-mortem.'

Angel leaned over the body and looked at the man's neck. He could see the two red marks of the snake's fangs and the angry red spot where the venom had been pumped in.

His lips tightened. He shook his head and rubbed his chin.

Mac saw him and said, 'Aye. It would have been very, very painful, Michael.'

Angel glanced at him and nodded.

Mac said, 'Aye, and instant paralysis might also have occurred. It isn't far from the neck to the brain, you know.'

Angel nodded. 'If the victim was so incapacitated, who played the music box *after* the snake had bitten Logan and why? It had to be somebody who could float through walls without leaving any trace. Or a very remarkable snake.'

Both Taylor and the doctor nodded their agreement.

Angel suddenly said, 'I have an idea.' He turned to the door. 'Won't be a minute.' He dashed out of the door, down the stairs and out through the front door. It was great to see that it was daylight. The sun was shining. He followed the concrete path around the side of the house until he was directly under John Logan's room window. He looked around the garden beneath and found two indents in the earth around a clump of lupines. They were typical of the marks made by a ladder. The earth was moist around the holes so they were very recent. He gently looked around the roots of the lupines and other plants hoping for a footprint but there was nothing there.

He returned to John Logan's bedsit, told Taylor that he had found the ladder marks and instructed him to make plaster casts of them. Then he called out to Mac who was speaking on his mobile, 'Going now, Mac. Back to the station. Will wait to hear from you.'

Mac waved.

Taylor said, 'I'll phone you if anything interesting turns up.'

'Thank you, Don,' Angel said and he went downstairs through the front door and down the garden path towards his car.

Before he reached it. An unmarked police car pulled up behind it. It was DS Carter.

He went up to the car, got in and sat beside her. 'What you got, Flora? See anything of a ladder?'

'No ladders, sir,' she said. 'I only saw one car on the move. It was heading out of the estate.'

'Did you get the number?'

'I did better than that. I ran a check on him.'

'Did you stop him?'

'Couldn't catch him, sir. He was travelling in the opposite direction at speed.'

'What did Swansea say?'

'The owner/driver was a Theo Duffield. They gave me his address and his driving record, which isn't that good.'

Angel's eyes flashed with impatience. 'Come on, Flora. We're looking for a killer, not a traffic violator. Who is Theo Duffield?'

She looked directly at him and meaningfully said, 'Theo Duffield is a *teacher* at Bromersley Modern.'

Angel pursed his lips.

SIX

Angel parked the BMW on the clearing in front of Bromersley School among the other cars, and Flora Carter followed in her car close behind him. They went straight to the school office together. Helen Thickett was seated at her desk tapping on the keyboard of a computer. She looked up.

Angel asked to see Mr Duffield.

Helen Thickett frowned. 'Mr Duffield?' she said. 'He's in a meeting.'

Angel sighed heavily and said, 'Well, he'll *have* to come out of it, Won't he?'

The secretary's eyes opened wide and her mouth fell open.

'And I'd like to see Mr Mitchell, please,' Flora Carter said.

'I'm sorry,' Helen Thickett said, 'He's with him. They are making emergency plans until Workingfield sends us two replacement teachers.'

Angel breathed deeply then said, 'Tell them we need to see them *now*!'

'It won't do any good,' Helen Thickett said.

Angel glared at her and said, 'It's a matter of life and death. Tell them that.'

She stood up, turned round to the head teacher's office door, tapped on it and went inside.

Angel turned to Flora Carter and said, 'We've got to move fast on this case, Flora. As you are interviewing the teachers, see what connections there might be between Eveline Pierce and John Logan. I mean in any way at all.'

Flora nodded. 'I know what you mean, sir.'

The head teacher's door opened. Mitchell came out followed by Helen Thickett.

Mitchell looked at the inspector and the sergeant and said, 'At the same time as we are mourning the loss of our dear friend and colleague, John Logan, we have to keep the school operating as normal as possible. To that end, Mr Duffield is assisting me in putting together a temporary timetable. For the school's sake, I trust that you will permit us to finish it before breaking off for anything else?'

Angel said, 'Mr Mitchell, I happen to think that preventing the possible imminent murder of another teacher is more important than delaying the education of some of your pupils. I assume you'd go along with that?'

Mitchell looked shaken by Angel's comment. 'Yes. Yes, of course,' he said.

'Right, well will you kindly allow us to make our investigations without further hindrance?'

'Of course. Of course. How can I assist?'

Three minutes later, Angel and Duffield were sitting at the corner of a huge table in the middle of the school library, which had a sign on the door saying, "Lesson in progress/do not enter."

Angel said, 'Mr Duffield, where were you at four this morning?'

Duffield stroked his moustache and said, 'At home in bed, of course, why?'

Angel's forehead creased. 'And where were you at 5.45 a.m.?'

'The same, at home in bed, fast asleep. Why?'

'You have a black Ford Mondeo car, licence number YP06MMX?'

Duffield blinked and stopped stroking his moustache. 'Yes, why?'

'It was seen in the locality of Beechfield Walk at 5.45 this morning.'

Duffield's face went red. He looked away.

Angel could see that his thinking mechanisms were working overtime.

The inspector pressed the advantage. 'What were you doing in Beechfield Walk at 5.45 this morning? I mean the address I have for you is West Street, that's off Wakefield Road, the other side of town.'

Duffield rubbed his forehead with his fingertips. Then he looked up and said, 'No comment.'

Angel's face creased as he said, 'No comment implies guilt, Mr Duffield. You know that?'

'And I want to see my solicitor,' Duffield said. 'I am not answering any more questions until I have seen my solicitor.'

* * *

Theophilus Duffield, senior teacher of history and politics, was promptly transferred to Bromersley station accompanied by two uniformed officers in a police car. He was designated as "helping the police with their enquiries," and his solicitor, a Mr King was duly informed.

Angel returned promptly to the station and was in his office.

The phone rang. It was Detective Superintendent Harker. Breathily he said, 'Come up here, straightaway.'

Angel wrinkled his nose and sighed. It was no pleasure being called up to Harker's room. It would only be for the superintendent to wail about something he had neglected to do or something he should have done. He always got plenty of brickbats but never any bouquets. Angel fully understood (as it is in the army) that the senior officer was the king and the king was always right, furthermore, he must always be *seen* to be right.

Angel arrived at the top of the corridor, knocked on the door and walked in.

Harker was a shrivelled prune of a man with a head shaped like a turnip. He had very little hair but a few long strands of ginger or white wisps sometimes fell over his eyes.

His office was considerably warmer than the rest of the station, Harker had two fan heaters blowing warm air into the room and circulating the smell of eucalyptus. His desk was piled up with ledgers, books, letters, papers, envelopes, boxes of Laxido, paper tissues and packets of paracetamol.

'Ah, yes, Angel,' Harker said. 'Sit down. I have just got back from a seminar on drugs initiated by COBRA following that find by the coastguard on a yacht off the Lincolnshire coast. The investigators reported that the drug seized from that yacht was a new drug nicknamed Looloo. This does not have the dangerous side effects of hard stuff like cocaine. It's a sort of introductory drug. Its intention is to get younger people, children, even young children to take it. Seemingly, it makes them feel very self-confident and happy, but it also has the side effect of making the druggie feel very hot. Looloo permits them to parade in minimal clothes in the winter and not feel the cold.'

Angel wondered whether it could be seen as a virtue. Save a fortune on clothes. Solve the world fuel crisis. If we felt hot in cold temperatures by simply taking a pill!

'Looloo is very addictive,' Harker said. 'The drug dealers are attempting the distribution around children at schools. Their strategy is that once the children have found the apparent benefits of this Looloo they may be tempted to try harder drugs. This playing around with the brain is stupid and dangerous. There'll very likely be a legitimate business been taken over and used as a cover distribution point known only to druggies. It amazes me, that anything that sends you away with the fairies and plays havoc with your body appears to be in such great demand these days.'

Angel thought that some people he knew were already away with the fairies and they didn't need any Looloo pills.

'Now, Angel, we have got to stamp this out. If, in the course of your enquiries, you stumble over any characters distributing the stuff or taking it, I want to know about it.'

* * *

Angel returned to his office. He always found it uninspiring visiting Harker. Listening to him was always either boring or irritating. But he *was* the boss.

He looked down at the desk and saw a slice of cake on a plate. He smiled. It would have come from Cassie. He was getting used to this. He knew he ought to make a contribution to the cost of it. He reached out and broke a piece off the cake and put it in his mouth. He pulled out his notebook and was checking off what he needed to do next, when the phone rang. It was Mary.

'Are you all right, love,' he said.

'Yes, of course,' she said. 'There are two things, darling. I was thinking about Mario and all that trouble he had the other night. I was thinking it would be nice if we went back very soon to show support. It would help him rebuild his confidence.'

'Yes. All right, Mary. Would *you* like to book it?'

'All right,' she said. 'And the other thing is . . .have you noticed that there is no heat coming from the radiator in the kitchen?'

'No, but if that is the case, Mary, phone the gas board on that service number in the address book and they should come today or tomorrow and fix it. It won't cost us anything because after we had the new boiler put in, the entire system, boiler, thermostat, radiators, the lot are under warranty for a year, and that's not up until sometime in May. Won't cost us a bean. All right?'

Mary pursed her lips as if to make a silent whistle. 'That's a relief,' she said.

Angel smiled. 'Anything else, love?'

'No. See you at teatime then,' he said. Goodbye.'

Angel was pleased that although there was a minor fault with his central heating, he was adequately covered by the comprehensive warranty.

There was a knock on the door. It was Cassie. 'Excuse me, sir, but a Mr King, Mr Duffield's solicitor has arrived.'

'Right, Cassie, take him into Mr Duffield. He's in the interview room next door.'

'Right, sir.'

'And there's something else, Cassie,' he said as she was still clasping the door handle. 'Come in a minute.'

He couldn't remember what it was he wanted her to do. He thought of it as he was shaving that morning. Then it came back to him. 'Will you phone Bromersley Modern School, speak to the secretary and ask her if she'd be kind enough to send us a copy of the weekly timetable of the lessons of class 10Q, that's the class young Sahil Khan is in.'

'Yes, sir. Anything else?'

'No. Yes. Thank you for the cake. I should be making a contribution to the cost of it.'

'Wouldn't hear of it, sir,' she said and the door closed.

He wouldn't be leaving it at that. A cadet's salary isn't very much, particularly when compared with his. If Cassie is going to be providing cake regularly, she needed remunerating appropriately. He'd organise a rota or something when he wasn't so busy.

He reached to his inside pocket and took out his notes. They were neatly written on the backs of used envelopes. He rubbed his chin. He wondered what the motive for the murder of the two teachers was. Although there was about twelve years difference in their ages, they were both regarded as senior teachers. They both seemed conscientious and were not sitting back on their earlier successes. Children notice that in teachers, and the students' enthusiasm (if there was any at all!) wanes also. This is reflected in the examination results.

There was a knock at the door.

'Come in,' Angel called. It was PC Donohue in patrolman gear. He had been a policeman at Bromersley station almost as long as Angel.

'Can I have a word, sir?' he said.

'Come in, Sean. Sit down. Of course. What's the matter?'

'I saw something a bit unusual this morning. I told the inspector, he said it might be helpful if I told you about it.'

Angel blinked. This was curious. 'What is it?' he said.

'Well I was on a routine patrol on the road between Forest Hill and Bromersley town. I was coming to the bridge over the River Don by Bluebell woods, when a man who hadn't a stitch of clothing on him was walking on the bridge wall. Then he must have heard the car coming, so he quickly turned to face the river, stretched out his arms and dived in. I stopped the car on the bridge, got out and looked down at the water. And I saw him swimming down river. He was soon out of sight because the river turns sharply right and he was hidden by the bushes and trees on the bank. Anyway, I drove the patrol car a short way forward, parked it out of the way and managed to get over a wall and through a hedge onto the riverbank to where I thought he might be. But I couldn't see him. I had a bit of a look round and kept out of sight for a few minutes, but I never saw him again. He must have got out of the river and run into Bluebell Wood.'

Angel nodded. 'I saw him on Monday. Must be the same man. Will you describe him?'

'Big chap, must be six foot at least, decent physique, big shock of fair hair, and as naked as the day he was born.'

'That's him,' Angel said. 'Well thanks, Sean. I don't know what action to take but I'm pleased to be notified.'

'I can only think that he's missing from a mental hospital, sir,' Donohue said.

'I have no better suggestions,' Angel said. 'Thanks again, Sean.'

Donohue went out and closed the door.

Angel picked up the phone and dialled one digit.

‘Control room. Sergeant Clifton,’ a voice said.

‘Ah, Bernie, have you had any reports at all from an ordinary hospital or a secure hospital or anywhere for that matter, of a man, possibly a patient, running off?’

‘No, sir. You asked me that on Monday.’

‘I know. There’s been another sighting. Sean Donohue saw him this morning. Somebody should have missed him by now.’

‘Sorry, sir. Nothing reported here.’

‘Right, Bernie,’ he said. He replaced the phone. It rang immediately. He snatched it up.

It was the cadet, Cassie Jagger. ‘Mr King says that his client, Mr Duffield is ready to be interviewed.’

* * *

Ten minutes later King, Duffield, Angel and a young detective, DC Edward Scrivens, the only one available from the CID office, made the foursome required to conduct a formal recorded interview. They were seated at a table in number one interview room.

‘Mr Duffield,’ Angel said. ‘Where were you at four this morning?’

‘I was with a friend of mine,’ he said, stroking his moustache.

‘What is the name and address of the friend?’

Duffield looked at King, then King looked at Angel. ‘Mr Duffield is concerned for the reputation of the friend, Inspector,’ King said. ‘If it became general knowledge, it could appreciatively affect her career and indeed her life. Neither of them is guilty of committing these murders. Nor have they been involved in a crime of any sort. The revelation of their relationship to the media would for her be disastrous. He asks that if you insist on pursuing the question that you will treat the information as highly confidential.’

Angel ran the tip of his tongue across his bottom lip. ‘Are you married, Mr Duffield?’ he said.

'No. I was very happily married in 1990 but my wife died six years ago.'

'I'm sorry to hear that, Mr Duffield. Is the friend you are referring to a married woman?'

Both King and Duffield looked downward. Eventually Duffield said, 'Yes, technically. But it didn't work out. The man — the husband couldn't get it right. He couldn't get *anything* right. The marriage only lasted two months. She is in the process of getting a divorce.'

Angel said, 'Mr Duffield, we are only interested in finding the killer of Eveline Pierce and John Logan. The private lives of you and your friend are of no concern of ours, provided that neither of you are engaged in any criminal activity. You may be relieved to know that most of what we uncover in a murder case is ditched because it has of no relevance to the case. If the information you are about to give me has no relevance to these murders, or any other crime, it will be ditched. It will certainly not be published by us or revealed in the trial.'

Duffield looked at King who nodded and muttered something. Duffield thought a moment then nodded and said, 'All right.'

King looked across the table at Angel and said, 'My client is ready to answer your questions, Inspector.'

Angel nodded and turned to Duffield and said, 'What is the name and address of your friend?'

'It is Emily Parkhouse. She's the art mistress at the school. Her address is 16 Oakfield Walk.'

Angel nodded. He knew it was only round the corner from John Logan, who had been lodging on Beechfield Walk.

'And were you in her company at from say, midnight until you were seen in your car?'

'I was with her from about six o'clock last night until around 5.30 this morning.'

'And do you expect Emily Parkhouse to confirm that?'

'Well, it's the truth. I expect she will.'

'You were seen in your car this morning at 5.45 a.m. in the locality of Beechfield Walk, what were you doing?'

'I would be on my way home . . . that is to 72 West Street.'

'Thank you, Mr Duffield.'

* * *

Angel ended the interview at 1.25 p.m. He had to release Theophilus Duffield who made it post haste back to the school.

Angel was quickly running back the recording of the interview, and PC Scrivens was tidying up the chairs.

'I know that chap Duffield, sir,' Scrivens said. 'It came back to me. You know when Mr King said that Duffield was worried if it got out that he was having it off with Emily Parkhouse, it would damage *her* career?'

Angel nodded thoughtfully.

'Well it came to me,' Scrivens said with a grin, 'it wouldn't do *his* career a lot of good neither. It's well known that Duffield wants to be the new headmaster, well, they call them head teachers now, at that new school, Headlands.'

'That's very illuminating, Ted,' Angel said. 'I must get off.'

* * *

Angel was in a small interview room next to the head teacher's office at Bromersley Modern School. He had his pocket recording machine on the table in front of him.

There was a knock on the door.

'Come in,' Angel called.

A woman about 35 years of age came in. She had big eyes that she exaggerated by flickering her eyelashes when he looked at her directly. She was surprised when she saw Angel in the room.

He stood up. 'Miss Parkhouse?' he said.

'I'm sorry,' she said. 'There must be some mistake? I had a note from Mr Mitchell to come to the interview room urgently.'

'Yes, Miss Parkhouse, it was to see me. Please sit down.'

She frowned. She wasn't happy. 'I can't stay long. I've left my class in the charge of a prefect. You're that policeman who is investigating the deaths of Miss Pierce and Mr Logan?'

'That's right. I have just come from interviewing Mr Duffield and I'd like to ask you a few questions, particularly in regard to your relationship with him.' He pointed to the recording machine. 'Do you mind if I record this, saves writing it all out.'

Her eyes flashed. 'Can't see what there is to record. How am I involved in the tragic deaths of those two people?'

'Let's see,' he said, switching on the recorder. 'Allow me to put a question first. Where were you at four this morning?'

'In bed, of course, asleep.'

'Were you alone?'

She breathed in noisily, looked Angel up and down and said, 'As you know the answer, why ask the question?'

'Were you in bed *alone*? It is necessary for you to answer the question in your own words.'

'I was in bed with Theo Duffield. *There*!' she said. 'Is *that* what you wanted?'

She was red in the face, her shoulders were raised, her lungs were full, her mouth was open, she was ready for battle.

'And where were you at 5.45 a.m.?'

'I was in bed alone. Theo had brought me a cup of tea and left at about 5.30.'

Angel nodded. His eyes narrowed. That meant that Duffield and Emily Parkhouse had an alibi. It would have been better for them if they had had an independent witness, he was thinking, but you can't have jam all the time.

'I hope you are going to keep that information confidential, Inspector,' she said. 'It could do untold harm to Theo's career if it was bandied about. And the children are quite wicked if they smell the slightest liaison between teachers.'

* * *

As Duffield seemed to be in the clear, Angel made it post haste back to Bromersley Police Station and when he was in his office, he pulled out the telephone directory of his desk drawer and found the number of Glover, G., and tapped it out on the phone.

It was soon answered.

'Good afternoon, Inspector Angel here. I wonder if you can help me?'

'I'll try, Inspector,' Glover said. 'I'm flattered to be asked.'

'I understand that a new school is being built in Bromersley.'

'Yes, Headlands, a massive new construction, on Pontefract Road. It will be finished and ready to open in about three months. I wouldn't want to live round there.'

Angel grinned. Then he said, 'Has the head teacher been appointed, do you know?'

'I don't think so. I have heard secretly, and confidentially, that our Theophilus Duffield has applied. But the governors of Bromersley Modern have heard nothing from him as yet.'

Angel smiled knowingly.

'How will Headlands school affect Bromersley Modern?'

'Only, I think in the finding and appointment of teaching staff. Teachers may prefer a large new modern building. It's for a thousand pupils, you know. It will offer more opportunities to the profession.'

'Have you not thought it might make it more difficult to replace the two who have been murdered.'

'I'm sure it will. They were both excellent teachers.'

'Thank you for that, Mr Glover. That has been most helpful. Goodbye.'

* * *

Angel arrived home at 5.10 p.m. He let himself in by the kitchen door. There was no sign of Mary or anything cooking. He went straight to the kitchen radiator and felt it. It was stone cold. He wrinkled his nose. He went into the hall and felt that radiator. That was lukewarm.

'Mary!' he called. 'Mary! Anybody home?'

'In the bedroom,' she called. 'Down in a minute.'

'Right,' he said. He went into the sitting room, glanced at the sideboard for any post. He saw an A4 sheet of paper with the gas company's logo at the top. It was partly printed and partly handwritten. He snatched it up and read it at speed. It seemed to say that an engineer had called that day at 2.15 p.m., examined the radiator and the boiler system but was unable to repair the kitchen radiator at the time.

Mary appeared all dolled up but in a dressing gown. She came up to him and kissed him on the cheek. 'Oh, I see you've found it,' she said.

'Hello, sweetheart,' he said quickly then he waved the paper and said, 'What's all this?'

'You've to ring them in their working hours on that 0800 number at the bottom. It's a big job, apparently.'

'What do you mean a *big* job?'

She looked at him impatiently. 'Leave it for now. The office is closed. You can't do anything about it until the morning. Put it out of your mind. We are going out to Mario's. I rang Valerie. The only night we could get our usual table this week was tonight. So I booked it. I hope that's all right.'

'Yes, that's fine,' he said. 'So that's why you look good enough to eat.'

She smiled. 'I have pressed your new suit,' she said. 'It's on a coat hanger in the bathroom.'

SEVEN

Michael and Mary Angel arrived in a taxi at Mario's at 6.55 p.m. on the dot. It left them nice time to leave their coats at the cloakroom, order a drink and arrive at their table for seven.

When they were seated, Angel looked round. He was pleased to see that the restaurant was filling up with customers and that the incidents they witnessed two days earlier had not seemingly affected Mario's business.

Across the room in the cubicle directly opposite, Angel noticed a woman in a low-cut pink frilly dress. He thought he recognised the face, but it was heavily plastered with paint and powder. She was peering round the velvet curtain, looking round the room and sipping from a glass.

He turned to Mary, and nodding towards the woman across the room, he said, 'Do you know who that is, in pink, on her own with a glass in her hand?'

Mary looked. 'No idea. Never seen her before.'

Then a tall man arrived, in a smart suit. The face of the woman in pink lit up. It was Gordon Glover. He leaned down to speak to her. The woman reached up and kissed him. He reciprocated, then suddenly pulled away and looked around the restaurant to see who might have seen them.

Angel turned away. He didn't want Glover to see that he'd been observing them. It dawned on him that the woman in pink behind that make-up must be, indeed was, Helen Thickett.

'That's Gordon Glover, the farmer, if that helps,' Mary said.

'Yes. I've met him,' he said. 'A farmer, did you say?'

'Yes. A gentleman farmer. He's considered quite a dish. He's very courteous. I'm told the girls in the library swoon when he comes through the door.'

Angel smiled.

'He's had a rough old life though.'

'Oh?' he said, trying not to sound interested.

'Lost his son. The boy took his own life. That's probably why he's so good as a school governor.'

Angel pursed his lips. 'Poor chap,' he said. 'Nobody should ever have to live through the death of their own child.'

'Then his wife left him.'

'I didn't know all that,' Angel said pulling his head into his chest and looking at her. 'Surprising what you learn in the public library.'

'They reckon he could charm the birds off the trees.'

A waiter arrived with two huge menus.

* * *

Although Angel had been anticipating some drama there that evening, it actually never happened. The meal was delicious. And so was the wine. And so was the music from the quintet. At around half past nine, Angel and Mary stood up, came out of the cubicle and were making their way through the tables to the door, when Angel felt a tap on his shoulder. It was Mario Giannini.

'Very nice to see you here, Inspector and Mrs Angel,' he said. 'I thought after Monday night's series of disasters, you wouldn't be back so soon.'

'Thank you, Mario,' Mary said. 'It's been a most pleasant evening. And the food was delicious.'

He beamed. 'Sank you, Mrs Angel. Sank you very much.' Then he turned to Angel and said, 'Have you managed to find any evidence proving zat Dorothy and zat waiter, Flagg were responsible for the events here on Monday night, Inspector?'

'No, Mario, but I have an officer working on it full time.'

'Ah. Good. Sank you. Sank you very much. Safe journey home. Good night, Inspector.'

Angel went to the kiosk and paid the bill to Valerie who was very sweet and courteous. He pocketed the paid bill and looked round for Mary. He saw her ahead of him at the cloakroom counter. She was talking to a couple, a pretty young woman he didn't know and a man with his back to him. As he approached them he recognised the man. It was Lance White.

Angel wasn't pleased that Mary was so friendly with him.

White turned and noticed he was coming towards them.

'Hello, Michael,' White said. 'Fancy seeing you here.'

'Good evening, Lance,' Angel said, not meaning a word of it. 'We were just leaving.' Then he looked at Mary, hoping that she would take the hint.

Instead, she said, 'What do think, Michael? Lance has introduced me to his partner, Dawn.'

The young woman pushed her right hand forward and said, 'Pleased to meet you, Michael.'

Angel brought up his hand and shook the small, cold hand and said, 'And pleased to meet you, Dawn.'

He put on a polite smile, looked at Dawn then turned back to Mary.

'Dawn is the bar manager at the Three Horseshoes on the corner of Mansion Hill and Rotherham Road,' Mary said.

'Oh, great,' Angel said, trying to sound enthusiastic. But he was thinking, what a boring and uninteresting life she was having.

Mary said, 'And *why* do you think they're here?'

Angel was thinking probably to celebrate breaking into another safe somewhere and stealing the contents, but he said, 'No idea.'

Mary looked at White and said, '*You* tell him, Lance.'

White stepped forward and said, 'We are going to get married, Michael.'

'Congratulations,' Angel said. Then he looked at Mary hoping that they could now break away, get a taxi and go home.

'Isn't that great news, Michael?' she said.

'Yes,' he said grabbing Mary's hand and giving it a telling squeeze. 'But we have to go, mustn't leave *your mother* on her own any longer. She'll be worrying where we've got to.'

Mary hesitated a moment. 'Oh. Er yes,' she said. 'My mother.'

Having made the break, Angel then dragged Mary up to the cloakroom counter and presented the ticket for their coats. As he helped Mary on with hers, he looked back at the open restaurant doors. Lance White and Dawn were already lost in the melee of people arriving, leaving or just hanging around.

Angel wondered how White, existing on social security and a bit of cash in hand for work on the side, could afford to dine at Mario's.

* * *

It was Thursday morning, 7 April.

Angel was in his office in his swivel chair looking across his desk at DS Taylor.

Between them, on the desk was a double sheet of bubble wrap and a ragged sheet of brown paper retrieved from the waste bin that had been in John Logan's flat.

'Absolutely no prints, sir,' Taylor said. 'The parcel must have been made up by somebody wearing gloves.'

Angel's face looked as if he had caught the pong of the fish pie in the cookhouse at Strangeways.

'Have you had the graphologist's report?'

'Yes, sir. It's here,' Taylor said as he unfolded a letter. 'It says "The writer gives little away because the entire address is in block letters. All I can say is that the writing is from a right-handed man probably middle-aged who is very confident."'

The information didn't bring any cheer to Angel.

'Were the post office at all helpful?' he said.

'No, sir. The cancellation stamp was over-inked so it was not possible to detect its number or any of the address.'

Angel looked down and rubbed his fingertips across his forehead. 'All right, Don. Thank you.'

Don collected the bubble wrap and brown paper wrapping from the desk and rushed out.

Angel looked down his list of jobs to do and came across the note to contact the gas company. He pulled a face, picked up the phone and tapped in the 0800 number. A recorded voice asked him to make choices and press buttons several times until he was eventually listening to a live human.

Angel told him the about the problem and gave him the Job No. on the sheet left behind by the fitter. The man quickly found the paperwork and simply said, 'Oh yes, sir. It is to arrange a date to flush your system out. Now that will take a whole day and will cost £600.'

'Oh no,' Angel said confidently. 'It won't cost us anything. We had a new boiler installed last May, and the entire system, boiler, thermostat, radiators, the lot are under warranty for a year, and that's not up for another month or so.'

'Ah yes, sir, that's right,' the gasman said, equally confident. 'Your new boiler, thermostat, switch controls and radiators *are* fully covered until May, but this trouble is in the pipes. You see your pipes must be quite old now and they have accumulated impurities which are blocking the flow of water to the radiators. The flushing out under pressure will free all that and you'll get much more heat for your money when it is done.'

Angel's face creased. 'But the pipes are covered by the warranty.'

'They are, sir, with this one exception. It's specified in the warranty. It's a standard clause. You will have received a copy of it and signed for it or else they wouldn't have gone ahead with the job.'

'I don't remember seeing it.'

'It's on the copy you have, sir, if you care to look. It had to be exempted from the warranty because it is such a big job. And it's the only exemption. It isn't included in the price because in some areas, where the water is different, it may need doing, and other areas it may never need doing at all. If you don't want it doing yet, sir, that's all right, but it needs flushing out before any quantity of those impurities reach the boiler and clog it up. Now *that* would be a *really* big job.'

Angel's muscles tightened. He felt stymied at every turn. He thought he had fully covered all the possible charges that could be made. He was particularly miffed because the only exemption from the gas company's 100 per cent warranty had to apply to him. 'I'll have to consider the matter,' Angel said. 'I will ring you back.'

He banged the phone back into its cradle. He knew he'd have to have the work done, and soon, but he needed time to acclimatise himself to the fact that in addition to the mortgage, he would owe £600 to the gas company. Also, he had to organise the payment of it. He was really put out. He thought that there couldn't be any additional charges coming his way for the safe delivery of the gas supply via the new boiler until May and then he was to be faced with this bill for the repair of the *only* fault in the contract (written in miniscule print) that was *not* included in the warranty.

He put it in the diary that later that day, he would have to phone the Northern Bank and organise the debt amount to be released to his cheque account and the sum added to the mortgage. Then he would have to contact the gas company and arrange a date with them to come and flush the system.

As he finished making the note, his phone rang. He reached out for it.

'Sergeant Clifton, sir,' the caller said. 'I am on the desk. Sorry to bother you, sir, but I have a boy, who is obviously a juvenile. He has been brought in by a man. The man accuses him of robbery. I can't get the lad to tell me his name. I can't make out a charge sheet without a name. I can't put him in a cell because of his age and if the man lets go of him, he tries to run off. I've run out of options . . .'

Angel wasn't pleased, 'Oh, Bernie, I've plenty on.'

'I'm sorry, sir. If there was anything else I could do, I would do it.'

'All right. I'll come down,' Angel said.

He walked in the charge room to find a burly man in denim trousers and a T shirt at the side of an Indian boy in a blazer and grey trousers. He was about fourteen of age. They were standing in front of Sergeant Clifton seated at a desk on a rostrum.

Angel went across to the group of two and said, 'I'm Inspector Angel, now what's all this about?'

'It's simple enough,' the man said. 'This lad broke into my car and stole a bar of chocolate.'

Angel said, 'I'm sorry to hear that, sir. What is your name?'

'Alexander Biggs. I work in the council tax office at the town hall.'

Angel nodded then looked at the sad face of the boy and said, 'And what is your name?'

The boy who had been looking at him, turned away.

Angel then looked up at the man and said, 'And what is the value of the stolen chocolate, Mr Biggs?'

'One pound 20.'

'And where was the car parked?'

'On the street, in front of our house.'

'And how much damage was done to the car?'

'Oh the car's all right.'

'You mean he didn't do any damage to it?'

'That's not the point. He broke into it.'

'But it *is* the point, sir,' Angel said. 'If he didn't have to trespass onto your property, and he didn't have to *force* an entry, in other words, if it was unlocked and he simply opened the door and went into it, then he didn't *break* into it.'

'You're playing with words.'

‘Not at all. If there’s no damage to the car, what harm has been done?’

‘It is at least burglary.’

‘Where was the bar of chocolate?’

‘On the dashboard.’

‘So it was clearly visible from the outside of the car?’

The man’s face was scarlet. He ran his hand through his hair. ‘Of course it bloody was,’ he bawled. ‘It had a sign on it saying “I am here to be stolen. Please break into the car and steal me. Thank you very much”.’

Angel rubbed his chin. He was pleased to see that the boy had been following the conversation. ‘And how do you know that this boy is the guilty one?’ he said.

‘Of course he was the guilty one. I was setting out for work at about half past seven this morning, I went to my car and noticed the windows were steamed up. I opened the door and found him asleep on the back seat. The chocolate bar wrapping was by his side.’

‘The chocolate would certainly be temptation to a boy,’ Angel said. ‘Particularly a hungry boy. So all you’re out of pocket is a bar of chocolate?’

‘Well, yes. But we want to stop this sort of hooliganism. We need to prosecute kids like this, on the streets all night. Drugged up to their ear holes, robbing and stabbing and raping. We hear about it every day. His parents should be ashamed of themselves.’

‘I agree with everything you have said, Mr Biggs, but this lad is guilty of nothing worse than taking a bar of chocolate when he was hungry.’

Angel turned to the boy and said, ‘Are you carrying a knife or anything with a sharp edge to it on you?’

The boy shook his head.

Angel was pleased. It was the first direct response he had had from him.

‘Do you take drugs?’

The boy shook his head violently.

Biggs' face went scarlet. 'You don't believe that, do you?' he said.

'As a matter of fact in this instance, I do,' Angel said. Then he turned to the boy. 'Roll up your sleeves and show me your arms, lad?'

The boy hesitated then he took off his blazer, handed it to Angel and rolled up his shirt sleeves. Then he thrust his arms up to Angel and twisted them round. Biggs was also looking on. They were clean and unmarked.

'Thank you,' Angel said to him, then held his coat while he slipped his arms in the sleeves.

He looked at the man and said, 'Are you satisfied, Mr Biggs?'

Biggs wrinkled his nose, muttered something unintelligible then said, 'No, I'm bloody well not. This boy entered my car uninvited and stole my chocolate.'

'He did,' Angel said. 'He did.' Then he looked at the boy and said, 'Is what Mr Biggs says the truth?'

The boy nodded.

Angel looked at Biggs and said, 'He pleads guilty. That's another thing we've found out. The boy isn't a liar.'

'If you want to proceed with the case against the boy, there's one thing you can be certain of, Mr Biggs, you'll win. This admission of guilt was in front of Sergeant Clifton and me. So we'll be witnesses for the prosecution. So if you can attend court this morning, with your solicitor, the case will be—'

Biggs' eyes flashed. 'I'm not setting on a solicitor,' he said. 'I can't afford to be—'

Angel quickly interrupted him and said, 'You'll get the expenses incurred in employing him from the defendant, that's this lad. Provided he has the funds of course. Actually I don't think he has any money.' He turned to the boy and said, 'Have you any money, lad?'

The boy shook his head.

Biggs noticed the time on the clock over the door to the reception area. It said ten past ten. His eyebrows shot up. 'Oh. Look at the time. I've wasted long enough on this and—'

Angel said, 'If you intend to proceed, Mr Biggs, you or your solicitor will need to be in the magistrate's court in about an hour to present your case against this boy.'

Biggs ran his hand through his hair and said, 'Oh it's bloody useless. I've more to do with my time than hang about a court all day for the price of a bar of chocolate. This isn't a police force. It's a kids' nursery.'

'We try to do our best for everybody, Mr Biggs.'

'Well, you haven't done your best for me!' he roared and made for the door.

'I thought we had, sir.'

The door slammed.

'We've saved you time and frustration,' Angel called after him.

But it was too late.

Angel and Clifton exchanged glances and smiled.

Clifton said, 'Thank you, sir. I couldn't have dealt with it like that.'

Angel smiled, looked down at the boy and said, 'Are you hungry, lad?'

The boy shook his head, then licked his lips.

Angel said, 'Thirsty?'

He nodded. Then Angel had an idea. He would try a question that couldn't be answered with a simple nod or shaking of head.

'Do you want tea or coffee?'

He didn't hesitate. He said, 'Coffee, please, sir.'

'Come on, then,' he said and Angel and the boy went out of the charge room along the corridor down to his office. As he reached the door, Cassie was coming out of it and closing the door. She was holding a folded sheet of paper.

'Oh, there you are, sir,' Cassie said. She looked at the boy and smiled.

'This is a friend of mine,' Angel said, looking at him. 'This is Cassie, she helps me.'

Cassie held out her hand. The boy hesitatingly held out his hand. They shook hands.

She said, 'Pleased to meet you.'

The boy nodded.

Cassie turned to Angel and said, 'I've been looking for you for ages, sir. I tried to phone you but you weren't in your office and you didn't answer your mobile.'

'I was in the charge room, Cassie. Anyway, what is it that's so urgent.'

'But you *never* go in the charge room, sir. It was a confidential message, so I wrote it down. I hope you can read my writing.'

Angel opened the note. It read: 'Mrs Khan phoned at 8.40 a.m. She said that she wanted to speak to Inspector Angel on an extremely urgent matter. Would you ask him to phone me on 833566 as soon as possible?'

Angel folded the paper and said, 'Thank you, Cassie.' Then he added, 'Would you bring us two coffees, please?' He turned to the boy and said, 'Do you take sugar?'

'Two, please, Cassie,' he said.

Angel concealed a smile of delight as he heard him speak.

'Right,' she said and she went off.

Angel looked down at the boy and said, 'This is my office, Sahil. Come on in. I've a phone call to make.'

The boy's eyes flashed. He looked closely at Angel and said, 'How is it you know my name?'

Angel closed the door. 'Sit down,' he said. 'I'm a detective. It's my job to know everybody I come in contact with. Besides your mother is very worried about you. That's what was in the note. She misses you. She wants me to phone her.'

Sahil looked down at the burgundy and grey coloured tiles on the office floor in an unfocused gaze.

Angel reached out for the phone and tapped in 833566.

The phone was answered immediately. 'Oh thank you, Inspector for phoning me,' Mrs Khan said.

The woman was obviously very worried.

Sahil carefully watched Angel's face, trying to follow what his mother was saying.

'The least I could do,' Angel said.

'My husband told me about you,' she said. 'May peace be with you. I am very worried about my son, Sahil. He was not in his bed when I called him for his breakfast. The last time I saw him was late last night. He has obviously sneaked out in the night. I have no idea where he is. He is not at school again. I have to report him missing. Could you please find him? I am out of my mind with worry.'

'Worry no more, Mrs Khan,' Angel said. 'Sahil is here, with me now. He's fine.'

It was difficult for her to believe. 'Oh! Oh!' she said. 'God be praised.'

'He has had a rough night, Mrs Khan.'

'Oh dear, is he in trouble?'

'I don't think so. Would you like to collect him?'

Suddenly, Sahil stood up. 'I'm not going back! I don't want to go back there and you can't make me.'

Mrs Khan said, 'I heard that, Inspector. Oh dear. That's what we are up against. Anyway, I'll be there shortly. Peace be with you.'

Angel replaced the phone, turned to the boy and said, 'Sit down, Sahil, and tell me what's the matter.'

'I am old enough to look after myself, sir. I don't want to go back home. They are making me do things I don't want to do. I am not their skivvy. When I'm old enough I want to get a job and make my own way.'

Angel peered at him closely. 'Hold on a minute, Sahil. What do they make you do?'

'Well, all sorts of things. Run errands. And when they're shorthanded in the restaurant, my dad sets me on with jobs.'

'What sort of jobs?'

'Preparing pineapples and stuff, folding napkins, checking and filling the salt and pepper pots . . . rotten little jobs . . . whatever needs doing. There's no skill needed. Anybody could do them.'

Angel could see it was going to be difficult. He rubbed the back of his neck. 'Don't you want to try to repay your mother and father,' he said, 'for bringing you into this world, and feeding you, clothing you, sheltering you and organising and supporting you through your education?'

'I didn't ask to be born. Anyway, all parents do that.'

'*Many* parents do that, but millions don't, either because they are ill, or stupid, or drunkards, or druggies, or thieves, or simply bone idle. You are lucky. Your parents have good health and they care. If your parents were idle, your father wouldn't have a restaurant. He'd probably have nothing worthwhile. He'd waste his time watching television or backing horses while drawing unemployment money or sick pay, trying to see how he could extricate more benefits out of the welfare state. He wouldn't worry about his children. His kids could please themselves about bunking off school. It wouldn't matter to him that his kids didn't have a good education and finished up as closet wallopers, washing public lavatories, or as dustbin men, emptying rubbish bins on the minimum wage for the rest of their lives. So Sahil, you want to think yourself lucky that you have the opportunity to help your father and mother now and again.'

'Well I don't mind helping now and again, I suppose . . . But it's the future.'

'What about the future?'

'They've got it all planned out. I have to go to university and study human resources and food technology, then join dad in the restaurant business and assist him to expand and open a chain of restaurants. And get married to a girl I have never even seen.'

'That's your parents plan for you, Sahil. And it sounds like a good plan. But plans have a way of going wrong.'

Sahil screwed up his face. 'How do you mean?' he said.

'Well, your parents are making lots of . . . assumptions. It's understandable. *Everybody* does it.'

'Like what, sir?'

'Hmmm,' Angel said. He shuffled his feet, rubbed his chin with his fingers. 'Well, they are endless. If you or your mother or your father were knocked down by a bus and died, that would upset the plan in a major way, wouldn't it? Supposing there isn't a place for you at a university for the subjects you need. Supposing that fast food and home delivery of readymade meals flourishes and the demand for dining out declines? Restaurants might become wholly unprofitable. Like email and credit cards have seriously affected the post office and the high street generally. I could go on. Those particular events will probably never happen. I just mention them as examples. Many unexpected events could easily upset the plan your parents have made for you. You should try to learn to live a day at a time.'

Sahil tilted his head and half closed his eyes. 'I think I understand that. But I want to be a vet, and work in a zoo. *They* want me to run a café.'

'Being a vet sounds like a good job. Mind you, there aren't many zoos around.'

'And I want to choose a wife for myself. That tradition of picking out a bride and bridegroom and agreeing the dowry when the couple are infants is outdated.'

'I know, but your mother and father don't think so. Anyway that marriage is years away. Remember what I said, a day at a time.'

There was a knock at the door. It was Cassie with two mugs of coffee.

After she had gone and they had sipped the hot coffee, Angel said, 'How are doing at school?'

'I hate it. I want to leave and get a job.'

'If you did that you wouldn't be able to go to university.'

He shrugged his shoulders. 'Everybody says that. I don't care.'

'You'd say goodbye for the rest of your life to ever becoming a vet.'

'I wouldn't have to run a restaurant for the rest of my life either.'

Angel's facial muscles tightened. 'Isn't that cutting off your nose to spite your face?' he said. 'I tell you, Sahil, if you left school now, you'd go straight onto the unemployment register. There are no jobs for unskilled fifteen-year-olds, and your unemployment money wouldn't even pay for your keep.'

'I would find something. I could live at home.'

'And sponge off your parents?'

'That wouldn't be sponging. They're my parents, I mean . . .

'You'd have the blatant cheek to defy your parents by abandoning all the plans and dreams they had for you by choosing to join the ever-increasing pool of unemployable, unskilled teenagers then expect your parents to *subsidise you*!'

Sahil shook his head. 'I could always work in the restaurant for my keep.'

Angel smiled. 'Well then, why don't you stay at school, go to university, get qualified and then if you don't get your own way, you can work in the restaurant in a *managerial* position. You'd be in a much stronger position than if you leave school early.'

Sahil's face showed Angel that he was thinking through what the detective had said to him. After a few moments, Sahil exhaled, looked upwards and smiled.

Angel thought that Sahil was accepting what he had said to him. He was excited both *with* him and *for* him.

Angel said, 'Listen to me spouting on about what the situation might be five or six years away. Things could very well change. There are a million permutations of what might happen. By that time, you might be well on your way to being a vet.'

Sahil's face brightened. 'Do you really think that's possible, sir?'

'Of course it's possible, but I shouldn't aggravate your parents now arguing about what might happen in five or six years' time. You, and they, but don't say I told you, are only arguing about something in the future that may never happen, and therefore you are simply aggravating each other unnecessarily. All right?'

Sahil nodded and grinned.

It did Angel's heart good to see him grinning.

'Now about school, Sahil,' he said. 'School is a necessary evil to be endured and to be worked at, if one seriously wants to become a professional man. In your case, a vet.'

Sahil nodded.

'School or college subject courses are planned rather like building a house and every lesson you miss would be like a brick missing from the finished building. I suggest that whenever you feel like bunking off, you say to yourself, if I miss this lesson there will be a hole in a wall of my house. I must hang on in there. Can you do that, Sahil?'

'I will try, sir.'

The phone rang. It was Cassie. 'Mrs Khan is here, sir,' she said. 'She's in reception.'

'Come in and take Sahil up there, will you?'

EIGHT

Later that morning there was a knock on Angel's office door. It was DS Carter.

'I've finished interviewing all the teachers at the school, sir,' Flora said. 'Have you a few minutes, sir?'

'Come in and sit down, Flora,' Angel said. 'I have as much time as it takes.'

'It won't take long, sir,' she said. 'I haven't that much to report.'

Angel's eyebrows went up. 'Oh,' he said. He had been hoping that she would have some information that would have produced new lines of inquiry.

She sat down, opened up her notebook and said, 'You particularly wanted me to see if I could find a connection of any kind between Eveline Pierce and John Logan. Well, I couldn't, sir.'

Angel pursed his lips.

'There were twelve teachers altogether,' she said. 'Everybody seems to have disliked John Logan. He was a bully to the children as well as the teachers. He had been known to handle the children, particularly some of the boys in short trousers far too boldly. I was told by Miss Parkhouse who was told by one of the girls that Logan used to pull up the boys' trouser legs at the back then pretend to nip the fleshy part of their buttocks. This was done in front of the class as a joke. Never — as far as anyone knows — was it done privately. It seems to me that he was very lucky not to be reported.'

'Extremely lucky. Any particular boy enrolled for that nonsense?'

'Apparently Sahil Khan was one of Logan's regulars.'

Angel's eyes creased. He ran his hand over his mouth.

Flora said, 'Also it was known that he had applied for the head teacher's position at that new school Headlands.'

Angel nodded. 'What about Eveline Pierce.'

'She wasn't much liked either, sir. She kept herself to herself. Some of the other teachers thought it was very likely that she had also applied for the headship of Headlands, but they really didn't know.'

Flora then closed her notebook and said, 'And that's it, sir.'

Angel's jaw dropped. He was expecting a lot more.

She sensed his disappointment.

Angel said, 'Did you sense that anyone knew about or had an interest in snakes or reptiles . . . or animals in general?'

'No, sir. The teachers, of course, expressed shock at the thought of the presence of venomous snakes in their bedroom and on their beds, but nobody expressed an interest in snakes or any other animals.'

Angel squeezed the lobe of his ear as he said, 'And the only relationship between the death of Eveline Pierce and John Logan is that they both worked at the same school, and that probably both have applied for the job as head teacher at Headlands.'

'Securing that position is surely not a strong enough motive for anyone to commit two murders, sir?'

'Not for normal, well balanced people, Flora. But not everybody is normal and well balanced.'

She considered his reply, nodded and said, 'Anyway, how do you get a snake to bite someone to order?'

Angel frowned. 'Don't know, but if you starve the snake, make it really hungry, angry and desperate, present it to an unguarded warm human being, I suppose it would very likely react violently.'

'Yes, but then how would you get it to return to you?'

'I'm not an animal trainer, Flora. But I imagine the anticipation of its favourite food would do it.'

'What *is* a snake's favourite food, sir?'

'According to Dr Mac, young rats and mice, preferred alive, because they enjoy killing them, but they also enjoy dead lizards, dead birds and bird's eggs as long as they are all fresh.'

'Uh,' Flora said, opening her mouth and pushing her tongue slightly forward. She shuddered and said, 'How perfectly revolting.'

He looked straight ahead, his eyes unfocussed, his eyebrows lowered and said, 'There's something else, Flora. As things are, we have no evidence to show that a human entered the bedrooms of the victims. Yet in both cases the music boxes were played. That's a real puzzle, Flora.'

'It's beyond me, sir,' she said.

'Anyway, *why* would they be played?' he said. 'They could hardly have been played to call for help. The deed had been done. The victims were dead. And the murderer wouldn't want them played to draw attention to the murders. That only leaves the snake. Could a snake be trained to open and close a music box on cue?'

'We don't know that the box was opened and closed at a pre-ordained time, sir. It could have been opened and closed by chance, by accident.'

'True, Flora. But what you say implies that it would be a coincidence.'

She nodded.

'Well, I don't believe in coincidences when it comes to crime and criminals,' he said. 'Don't see it as a coincidence. There *is* or *was* a reason for it to have happened.'

'And what's that, sir?'

'I wish I knew. The murderer would only be interested in getting the hell out of there, wouldn't he?

'You would think so.'

'So *why* were they played?' he said. His face muscles tightened and he ran his hand through his hair. 'We've never had a case like this. Can you imagine a man wearing thick gloves outside up a ladder up to a bedroom window in the dark, waving a rat or a mouse at the snake to persuade it to come out of the bedroom?'

'It sounds very erm . . . unlikely, sir.'

The phone rang. He reached out for it. It was Mary Angel. She didn't sound happy.

'What's the matter, love?'

'Oh Michael, the lights keep flickering. The radio goes off for a second or two then comes back on. Whatever is it?'

Angel's jaw dropped open. 'I don't know, love, do I? I'm supposed to be investigating—'

'There must be something wrong with the wiring . . .'

'The wiring? What could be wrong with the wiring? It's been all right for the twelve years we've lived there, hasn't it? Why should it suddenly—'

'That's the point. Maybe it's ready for re-wiring.'

His face went red. He squeezed the phone. 'It *doesn't* need re-wiring,' he said. He could visualise the cost of re-wiring and then decorating every room in the house. 'It's probably the electricity people switching things about.'

'They don't keep switching things about every ten or twenty minutes.'

'You don't know *what* they do. Might be some apprentices on the moors in the middle of nowhere, wherever our electricity comes from . . . having nothing to do . . . with time on their hands just playing around.'

'I don't believe it, Michael. It's something wrong here. In this house. And it wants seeing to.'

Angel's grip on the phone tightened. He ran his hand through his hair. 'Well, I can't do anything until I get home,

Mary. I'm sorry. By that time it will probably have put itself right.'

The call was ended without much grace on either side.

He turned back to the sergeant and said, 'Sorry about that, Flora. Where were we?'

'You were visualising the murderer standing on a ladder outside John Logan's bedroom window waving a rat about—'

'Oh yes. I think we can leave it there, Flora. I need to see Don Taylor about something.'

* * *

It was half past twelve.

There was a knock at Angel's office door.

'Ah, Don. Come in. Sit down.'

When Taylor was settled, Angel said, 'I've been reading your SOC report of the findings at Eveline Pierce's scene, and essentially your conclusions are that no other person had been in the room, and you don't put a time limit on it.'

'That's true, sir. No person had been in that room as far as our forensic ability was able to detect. There was no human residue anywhere in the room that wasn't from Eveline Pierce. There were no fingerprints or part prints that were not hers. Obviously there must have been some strangers in the room at some time. When the woman moved into to the place, the removal men, the painters and decorators and so on must have had access. But since that time, maybe ten or twenty years ago, the room had been cleaned, vacuumed maybe a thousand times and the furniture polished and/or wiped down by the victim, herself.'

'Am I to understand, therefore, that nobody entered the room the night she was killed?'

'That's a step too far, sir. But it's certainly true to say that if somebody did, they did not leave any residue. To be sure of non-detection, they would need to have been dressed in a sterile overall or similar, wearing gloves, and having their hair completely enclosed.'

‘Hmm,’ he said, rubbing his chin with his fingertips. ‘That’s not at all likely.’

‘The report on John Logan will be similar. Except of course, his housekeeper’s prints and residues are all over the room, as well as his own. But nobody else’s.’

Angel’s face creased. He rubbed his forehead and temple hard with his fingertips. After a few seconds, he said, ‘Right, Don. Thank you very much.’

Taylor went out.

Angel promptly picked up the phone. He was soon speaking to Dr Mac. He apprised him of the discussion he had just had with SOCO and then he said, ‘Would it be possible, Mac, or even likely, for Eveline Pierce and/or John Logan, both suffering from the bite of a poisonous snake, to have risen from their beds, reached out to their music boxes one or two metres away, played the music for half a minute or so, replaced them, then returned to their beds?’

Mac didn’t answer promptly. ‘Erm, well, Michael. It’s difficult. For one thing, there is no telling how much pain the human body can endure. And we all have different pain thresholds. If there was some vital reason why, despite the pressure on your heart, the faintness and the intense pain, you should play the music box because it would direct the cavalry where to charge to save you or others from certain death, well . . . you might do it.’

Angel said, ‘Yes, Mac. I take your point.’

Mac said, ‘Then again, if *I’d* been bitten by a snake, Michael, and I hadn’t immediately become comatose, I wouldn’t think for a second about the music box. I’d want to find a safe place where I wouldn’t be bitten again, and then I would be thinking how I could get some quick relief from the trauma.’

Angel nodded. It was exactly how he felt about it. But it left him with the still unanswered questions, who played the music box at the time the victims had been bitten, and why?

* * *

It was 5.20 p.m. when Angel drove the car into the garage, pulled down the door, locked it and made his way down the path along the side of the house to the back door. It opened straight into the kitchen.

Mary was busy with something in the sink as he went in.

'You're early,' she said, with a smile.

He went over and gave her a kiss. 'Well, on time,' he said. 'For a change.'

'You know you were better off when you were a sergeant.'

Angel looked down at what she was doing. She quickly lowered some dishes into a bowl of lathered water.

'What are you doing?' he said.

'What do you *think* I'm doing?' she said. 'Washing up. You've seen me do it a thousand times!'

He knew from her cold attitude that she was hiding something. He recalled that she didn't usually wash up the dirty pots from lunch because it wasn't worth the bother. The dirties from a beaker of coffee, a beaker of soup, some fresh fruit or a sandwich didn't amount to the pile she had just dumped in the water.

Angel deduced that she's had a friend or a relation for a meal. She would no doubt tell him in due course.

He reached in the cupboard for a glass tumbler, then into the fridge for a can of German beer. When he reached up to the shelf in the fridge door he noticed that there were only four cans, he took one out. As he pulled the ring and poured the beer into the glass, he remembered that he had opened a fresh pack of six the previous night. So there should have been five on the shelf. Somebody had had one. Mary disliked all beers and lagers, so she wouldn't have had it.

He sipped the beer. It tasted good.

'Tea will be about ten minutes, darling,' she said. He noticed she was all sweetness and light now. 'Would you like to set the table?'

He took out coasters and mats from a drawer in the chest, cutlery from under the worktop and salt and pepper from out of the cupboard. He began to set them in position.

Mary turned away from the sink and said, 'You haven't asked about the lights that were flickering.'

He looked up. He had forgotten about it. Although, if it had still been happening, he knew it would have been the first thing she would have mentioned.

'I suppose it's all right now,' he said. 'I told you it would go right on its own.'

'Ah,' she said, triumphant in what she was about to say. 'But it *didn't* go right on its own.'

Angel's face dropped. He didn't want another bill, particularly now that he had to pay the gas people an unexpected £600 for the forthcoming flushing out of the central heating pipes.

'You didn't ring the electricity board, did you?' he said.

He was dreading her answer.

'No,' she said. 'I rang the Three Horseshoes pub, where Lance White's girlfriend, Dawn, works. Asked her if he was there. He wasn't, but she said she could get in touch with him. Well, to cut a long story short, he came and fixed it in no time. And being lunchtime I made him a meal—'

He wrinkled his nose. 'And you gave him a can of my beer as well, didn't you?'

Mary's eyes flashed. She was really angry. 'Michael Angel, you really are the limit! That's *all* he had. Do you begrudge a man who has done us a service a meal and a can of beer? You should just be thankful that I didn't call a qualified electrician.'

All the muscles in Angel's body tightened. Then he sighed.

'I do wish you'd stop encouraging Lance White,' he said. 'I've told you. He's bad news and he's dangerous. I have no doubt he has some plan cooking to get his own back on me.'

Mary breathed in then exhaled loudly. 'It's always *me, me, me*,' she said. 'Aren't you pleased the fault was fixed? Are you so blind that you can't see that the man has changed, is repentant and trying to live a decent, useful life?'

Angel looked down and shook his head.

'I don't know how to convince you that this man is a recidivist, Mary,' he said. 'Furthermore, he believes that I deliberately betrayed him which resulted in him being put behind bars. I told him what really happened, but he was not convinced. Therefore he holds a grudge against me. I am sure he will retaliate at the first opportunity and you are making it easy for him by inviting him into our house and into our lives.'

'He's a really nice man when you get to know him, if you treat him decently he's responds positively,' she said as she rolled her shoulders.

Angel ran his hand through his hair. '*That's just an act*, Mary. He's *dangerous*! I could be Mister Wonderful for a day or a week or a fortnight. Anybody can. How can I get it into your thick head that he is a villain and he's dangerous.'

'Well, why don't you arrest him and wrap him up in barbed wire then?'

Angel breathed in noisily, snatched up his glass from the table and stormed out of the kitchen into the sitting room.

* * *

It had been a difficult evening for Michael and Mary Angel.

There had been long silences between them with occasional short, crisp spurts of questions and answers, such as, 'More coffee?' 'No thank you.'

In bed, it was as if Hadrian had been busy and built a construction right down the middle of it. And they did not converse over breakfast the following morning because Mary had stayed in bed feigning sleep. Angel had contented himself with the cut and thrust of John Humphreys and a Cabinet Minister fighting it out on Radio 4.

Angel arrived at the office at 8.28 a.m. On his desk he saw a piece of Victoria sponge cake on a plate. He eyed it while he took off his coat. So Cassie must be in. It's time he paid his way. He picked up the cake and took a big bite out of it. He wasn't going to wait until coffee break.

The phone rang. He reached out for it. It was Sergeant Clifton from the control room. Through the cake he mumbled a greeting.

'I thought you'd like to know, sir,' Clifton said. 'I have just heard on the wire. There's been a big robbery from a mill in Cubley Bottom. A hundredweight of that new drug, Zyxantium, commonly known as Looloo. They reckoned it had a street value of 4 million. Three masked men. Got away in a stolen bread van. Last seen on Cuckoo Road travelling in the direction of Bromersley.'

Angel hurriedly swallowed the last bit of the cake and said, 'Where's Cubley Bottom?'

'The other side of Huddersfield, sir,' Clifton said. 'Not on our patch.'

Angel sighed with relief. 'Thank goodness. We've enough on,' he said. Then, with his eyes half closed, he put his head on one side and said, 'Funny though, Three masked men in a *bread* van.'

'Yes, sir. And I didn't like the bit about travelling in the direction of Bromersley.'

'What time did you pick that message up?'

'Just now. I rang you straightaway.'

'Mmmm. Haydn Asquith won't know about this, Bernie. Would you advise him that I suggest that he sends out an urgent notice to all our mobiles to be on the lookout for three masked men in a bread van?'

'Right, sir.'

'It wouldn't do us any harm at all to look good for a change to our comrades in West Yorkshire, if this cop shop could do anything really clever, like picking them up would it, Bernie?'

Clifton grinned. 'No harm at all, sir.'

Angel replaced the phone.

He closed his eyes and gently rubbed his forehead with the tips of his fingers. He was thinking what a great coup it would be to pull in the local bigwig in the drug trade. It's about time there was some more good news about the place.

There was a knock at the door. He looked up.

'Come in,' he said. It was DS Crisp.

'Have you got a couple of minutes, sir?' he said.

The sergeant didn't look very happy.

'Yes, lad?' Angel said. 'Sit down. What have you got?'

'I know you are not going to be pleased about this, sir, but small disturbances are still happening in Mario's, and I have still not been able to find who is responsible. And, as far as the robbery of the £300 float is concerned, it looks impossible for it to have been stolen by any of the three suspects.'

'What sort of disturbances are you talking about?'

'Well, they've never stopped. Sauces and coffee and soup in the wrong jug or cup or container or whatever. Obviously to deliberately frustrate the waiters and upset the customers. Mario is always having to make apologies and give refunds.'

Angel scratched his head then ran his fingertips over his temple. 'Mmm. And what about £300 float?'

'It looks impossible for it to have been stolen by any of the three suspects.'

Angel rubbed his hand across his mouth and jaw. 'Why, lad? Explain it to me.'

'Well sir, the only people to have been anywhere near the pay desk the entire evening were Mario Giannini, Stefan Peruzzi, and Miss Valerie Downing. I have interviewed all three *again*. There is, of course, no reason for Giannini to be suspected. It was *his* money. For almost as good a reason Valerie Downing wouldn't make herself into such an obvious suspect, after all the float was entirely her responsibility. And I think that she was in such a strong position that she could have devised a far bigger scam than that if she had wanted or needed money.'

Angel nodded. 'And the man, Stefan something or other, the waiter?'

'Stefan Peruzzi, sir. He's a charming man. He's old. He's 65.'

Angel blinked. 'That's not old.'

'He looks old. He has no family. He's no longer married. He is on his own. He worked for Giannini's father and he's worked for Mario Giannini ever since he opened his first little café. Both Giannini and Valerie Downing speak highly of him and both insist that he wouldn't steal a currant, especially from Mario. He certainly *seems* to be the genuine article, and besides, he doesn't have a motive.'

Angel rubbed his chin for several seconds. 'Hmmm. This Peruzzi, Stefan Peruzzi, old faithful family retainer,' Angel said. 'Wouldn't harm a fly? Pure as the driven snow?'

Crisp face brightened. 'Yes sir. That's *exactly* it.'

Angel pursed his lips and with his eyes half closed, he said, 'And I suppose all three talk in highly respectable lovey dovey terms about the other two.'

Crisp smiled. '*Absolutely*,' he said.

Angel nodded confidently and said, 'Right. I think I know how to get to the bottom of this nonsense. Arrange a meeting here with me next Tuesday or Wednesday with Stefan Peruzzi and Valerie Downing.'

'Right, sir. What about Mario?'

'I definitely don't want Mario at that meeting. Just those two?'

'Well, who do you want to see first?'

'I want to see them both together, of course.'

Crisp frowned. Questioning suspects in groups of more than one was universally regarded as bad technique. '*Together*, sir?' he said.

Angel's lips tightened. He stared at him and said, 'Of *course*, lad. Of *course*!'

The phone rang. He glared at it.

He turned back to Crisp and said, 'Go on, lad. Get on with it.'

Crisp stood up. He didn't look pleased. 'Right, sir,' he said as he made for the door.

The phone was still ringing. When the door closed, Angel snatched it up impatiently.

'Hello, yes!' he said.

It was the inspector, his opposite number in the uniformed division of the Bromersley force. 'Haydn Asquith, here. What's up, Michael? I hope I'm not ringing you at a bad time?'

'No. Sorry, Haydn. Just trying to sort one of my lads out. What can I do for you?'

'This bread van. Just had a report that it was seen briefly on Church Street. Our patrolman was systematically looking down the streets, when he saw it. It was standing on the corner. It looked as it was parked up. Our patrolman had difficulty parking. He wanted to be somewhere where he could see them but they couldn't see him. He couldn't quite get the position he wanted, but nevertheless, he pulled up, switched on his VCR, got out his car, and approached the van on foot. As he got near, they must have seen him, started the engine and quickly drove off. By the time our patrolman got back to his car, the van was at the end of the street and out of sight. He'd lost them. Couldn't pick up a trail.'

'Too bad, Haydn, but a good try.'

'Yeah. I can tell you that it was a Towson bread van. Littlemore Street, Leeds. Stolen from outside their bakery, last night. Don't know what time. It wasn't missed until a quarter to six this morning. I've spoken to the night manager. They've got eighteen vans in red and white. All the same livery.'

'Yeah. I've seen them around. Better luck next time, Haydn,' he said. 'Thanks for the info.'

NINE

Angel left the station at five minutes to ten and drove the BMW into the centre of town. He was fortunate to find a parking place in a small area behind the town hall, and it was a short walk to the Golden Moon restaurant, which was on the main shopping street with some of the major chain stores nearby.

Through the large plate glass windows of the restaurant, he could see no sign of life, but many small tables and chairs set out as orderly and smart as a brigade of guards. The tables were covered with spotless tablecloths and bearing gleaming cutlery and glassware. He saw a neatly printed sign on the inside of the shiny glass door. It read: "Sorry, we're closed. Open at 11.30 a.m."

Nevertheless he tried the door. It was unlocked so he opened it and went inside.

A big man, built like a wrestler appeared silently from nowhere. He had oriental features and was wearing a short white coat. He said, 'Can I help you?'

He spoke as if he had just learned the phrase.

Angel introduced himself.

The giant nodded. He turned the key in the door to lock it then said, 'Follow me, please.'

Angel was directed through a line of tables, past the entrance and exit doors to the kitchen to another door. The man banged on it and pushed it wide open.

Khan was seated at a desk in a small smart office.

He stood up and touched his turban above his temples with his fingertips to check that it was properly in place.

'Ah, Inspector Angel, please come in, sir,' he said. Then he glanced across at the big man, said something unintelligible to Angel and the man went out and closed the door.

'May peace be with you, Inspector. Sit down, please.'

Angel nodded. 'Thank you. And may peace be with you, also.'

Khan said, 'I trust that you are not erm . . . erm . . .wanting to see me on a police matter. Everything that I do and everything my wife and Sahil do, I hope are beyond reproach.'

Angel smiled and said, 'Of course they are, Mr Khan. And by the way, how is Sahil?'

Khan said, 'Well, Inspector, sir, by the will of God, he is home and has attended school yesterday and, as I have heard nothing from my wife up to now, he must be at school as we speak. But he is difficult. Do you know, sometimes I think I am on the edge of a volcano waiting for it to erupt?'

Angel said, 'I have spoken to Sahil. We had quite a long talk together.'

'Really? He didn't tell me. He tells me nothing. That's also worrying.'

'He does not want to be in the restaurant business.'

Khan's face hardened. 'I know that. I didn't want to be in the restaurant business either, but my father directed me into it. I was not happy at the time. It was a miserable experience for me at the time, but now I see the wisdom of it. My family and I have wanted for nothing. I actually wanted to be a pilot in the commercial air transport service and fly all over the world.'

'Sahil wants to be a vet.'

'I know,' Khan said with a sigh. 'My wife got him a kitten, which he was delighted with until it grew into a cat then he lost interest in it and my wife finished up looking after it. Next thing was, he wanted a bearded dragon. I got him one of those recently. It costs me a small fortune in electricity, maintaining a large hot, glass tank for it day and night all the year round, to say nothing of the veterinary fees. I think it was when he saw how much vets could charge, that he became interested in the profession.'

'And he wants to be able to choose his own wife.'

'Don't we all?' Khan said looking closely into Angel's eyes. Then he added, 'I don't intend to justify that, Inspector. The arguments for and against have been well rehearsed, many, many times.'

'Indeed,' Angel said with a nod. Then he said, 'I believe I have also worked out why he did a bunk off school on Tuesday morning.'

'Oh? I would like to hear why, Inspector, sir.'

'Because according to the timetable of his class 10Q, on Tuesday morning, his first lesson is Latin, followed by double geography. The two subjects he hated. And they were taught by the two teachers who are now dead.'

Khan's eyes flashed. 'Ah. Inspector, sir. I did not know of the coincidence. He didn't tell me. He's so difficult. His mother can do more with him, but she couldn't get that out of him either.'

* * *

Angel returned to his office.

He was not a happy man. There were lots of ideas spinning around his thought processes. He didn't immediately notice the strawberry tart on a plate in front of him.

He had an uneasy feeling about the little man in the turban. He picked up the days post from the top of the pile on his desk, turned over each envelope and looked at it with unfocused eyes.

There was a knock at the door. He slapped the envelopes back to the pile and said, 'Come in.'

It was DS Crisp. He was looking pleased with himself.

'What is it, lad?' Angel said, expecting to be disappointed with whatever he was told.

'That meeting you asked me to set up here, in your office with that waiter Stefan Peruzzi and Valerie Downing. It's to be here next Tuesday at 3 o'clock. Is that all right, sir?'

Angel frowned at first, then remembered what it was about. He raised his eyebrows. 'O great stuff,' he said unenthusiastically. He reached out for his desk diary and made the entry.

Angel said, 'Sit down a minute, Trevor. I've another job for you.'

Crisp sat down on the chair nearest to the desk.

'Have you heard of a bearded dragon?' Angel said. 'I think they come from Australia.'

'Oh yes, sir. My brother had one . . . a few years ago now. I had to look after it when he went on his honeymoon.'

Angel brightened. 'Yes. Yes,' he said animatedly. 'What do they eat?'

'Mice, insects, some sort of worms and some vegetables, sir. I remember mashing up some carrot for my . . .'

'How do you feed them?' Angel said. 'Do you have to catch the mice?'

'There are some pet shops and specialist shops that sell mice live or dead.'

Angel frowned. 'Live or dead? Don't tell me they are fed to these dragons alive?'

'I'm afraid they are, sir. By some people. I don't believe it's necessary but . . .' Crisp shrugged.

Angel wrinkled his nose and shook his head to show his disgust. Then he looked up. Something interesting had occurred to him. 'That's a similar diet to snakes,' he said.

Crisp thought it was and nodded. 'I believe so.'

Angel wondered if he had sufficient justification to get a warrant to search Khan's house and his restaurant.

He looked up at Crisp. 'Find out if there is anything known about Rajveer Khan and Sahil Khan. Do it from CID and let me know ASAP.'

Crisp went out.

Angel looked round his desk and spotted the strawberry tart. He picked it up and bit into it. It was pretty good. He was thinking, he should pay for these little treats. He must sort this out with Cassie. He leaned back in his chair and finished it off. Then he wiped his hands on his handkerchief.

He was thinking about the motive for the two murders. If he could establish that, it would point up the possible suspects . . . people who had something substantial to gain from the death of Eveline Price and John Logan. He had already identified Rajveer Khan as a serious possibility. He considered that the son, Sahil, was too young to commit the murders on his own. Although he didn't entirely rule it out. There was the need to take a ladder, in the case of the murder of John Logan, that required a means of transporting it to the scene. A car or a vehicle of some sort would be needed for that purpose. Sahil was really too young to drive. Of course it didn't mean that he couldn't drive, or that he didn't drive. But, everything considered, Angel thought it unlikely that Sahil could have done such a thing on his own. But he could have been an accessory to his father.

If Crisp returns and says that Rajveer Khan is *not* known to them, Angel knew that he really wouldn't have sufficient justification to apply for a warrant to search his place.

He mused on.

He thought of Theophilus Duffield. In his case, the motive would have been to secure the position of the first head teacher of Headlands, one of the largest schools in the country. His alibi was that he was in bed with Emily Parkhouse. A perfectly satisfactory alibi, if it had been true. Of course, the pair of them could be in league together to reduce the competition for the position. But again, Angel hadn't justification to ask for search warrants of either of their homes.

All things considered, he felt that progress was remarkably tedious if not non-existent.

There was a knock on the door. It was DS Crisp.

Angel looked up eagerly. 'What have you got, lad,' Angel said.

'Rajveer Khan is *not* known to us, sir. Neither is Sahil,' Crisp said.

Angel pulled a disagreeable face, then breathed in and out noisily. He began to think that there was something he must have missed.

'Right, Trevor,' he said. 'Carry on with what you were doing.'

Crisp went out.

Angel rocked back in the swivel chair and stared with unfocused eyes at the ceiling. He stayed in that position for several minutes then leaned forward and reached for the phone. 'Ah, Don, have you got the keys to Eveline Pierce's bungalow?'

'I will have to check, sir. There was some discussion about what to do with them with her sister who lives in Preston.'

'She's her next of kin, I presume?'

'Yes, sir. Hold on. I'll have a look in the register.'

He came back in a few seconds. 'Yes, sir. They're here.'

* * *

Twenty minutes later Angel pulled up the BMW at 32 Bedfordshire Gardens, the last home of Eveline Pierce.

He noticed a For Sale sign stuck in the garden of the bungalow next door, number 30. He was sure he hadn't seen it before. It called to mind the occupier, Mrs Cowdrey, who had heard the music box playing in the early hours of the morning.

He walked up the garden path of number 32 to the front door. He noticed that the damaged door jamb had been replaced with new timber which needed undercoat and gloss to match the door. He inserted the key in the door lock. He opened the door and went inside. He saw some post on the mat. He bent down and picked it up. There was one important looking letter with a Workingfield post mark, and two colourful fliers advertising pizza and curry delivery services.

He closed the door, tossed the fliers on the hall table and opened the letter.

It was from the Education Appointment Department, Workingfield Town Hall. It was dated 4 April 2016.

It said:

Dear Miss Pierce,

Further to the position of head teacher at Headlands Community College, I am pleased to advise you that the committee has asked me to inform you that your application has been successful.

While your engagement at Headlands will be considered to begin on 1 September 2016, there will be several meetings necessary before that date to facilitate the smooth transition from your present post at Bromersley Modern School to establishing and becoming the first head teacher at Headlands Community College. I trust that that does not present a problem in any way.

Your early reply would be appreciated.

Yours sincerely,

Anthea Pickles

(Secretary Workingfield Education Committee).

Angel noticed that it had been posted on Monday of that week and he found it poignant that she should have been offered the job the day she was murdered.

He folded the letter up and put it in his pocket. Then he went down the hall to the bedroom where he hoped to be inspired by something — he didn't know what.

He stood outside the room where she had died. He noticed how quiet the bungalow was. All he could hear was the throbbing of his own heart. He opened the door and went inside. At first the room seemed exactly as it had done when last he was there, but there was a difference. A significant difference. It was fresher and cooler. He looked around. A curtain was quivering slightly. He immediately crossed to the window. He saw that a small pane of glass had been smashed and the catch unfastened. Somebody had broken into the bungalow since SOC had finished their work and uniformed branch had ceased protecting the premises.

He rubbed his chin hard. He mustn't touch anything.

He took out his mobile and summoned Don Taylor and the SOCO team. Then he toured the rest of the bungalow, carefully looking in big cupboards and behind large pieces of furniture, but there were no signs of anybody being present or that the other rooms had been entered or disturbed in any way. The intruder seemed only to have entered the bedroom.

He decided he would have a look outside the bedroom window where the intruder had gained entry. There were muddy marks on the black paint of the window ledge and a few splinters of glass on the path and the ledge, but that was all he could see. He didn't expect any forensic from that quarter.

He returned to the bedroom. Everything else seemed in order. If the dressing-table drawers had been opened, they had been very carefully closed, which would be unusual for a thief. They are in such a hurry that they do not usually close drawers. He glanced at the dressing-table top. There were the traditional items there and nothing else. *Nothing else*?

'Where's the music box?' he said.

The music box should have been in the centre of the tray.

He squeezed his eyes shut. His jaw muscles tightened. He wondered if it had been pushed into a dressing-table drawer by a thoughtless SOC man.

There were two drawers each side of the kneehole. He quickly reached into his pocket and picked out two 50p coins, and holding them one in each hand he put them around the knob of a dressing-table drawer and pulled it open. He remembered that there was the possibility of him disturbing a resting, poisonous snake. So he poked around inside, stabbing the contents with a pencil, but there was no music box. And thankfully no snake. He closed each drawer in turn after checking it by applying the coins to the knob.

He sighed, rubbed his chin and looked round the rest of the room.

Then he heard the banging of the front door knocker, the door opened and a voice called out. 'Are you there, sir?'

It was DS Taylor.

'Coming,' Angel called and he rushed out of the bedroom into the hall. There were standing DS Taylor and two PCs. They were all in their whites, masked up and carrying white packs and valises.

'The place of entry is through the window in the bedroom, Don.'

'Right, sir,' he said.

Taylor looked at the two PCs behind him and indicated with his thumb to get on with it.

'Was it robbery, sir?'

'I'm not sure. The music box isn't on the dressing table. Do you know where it is?'

Taylor frowned. 'It was dusted for prints then put back there, where it was found.'

Angel said, 'Well, it isn't there now.'

Taylor stepped into the bedroom and said, 'Do either of you know anything about the music box?'

They both replied in the negative.

Taylor said, 'I put it there myself, sir.'

'Right,' Angel said. 'Carry on then. See if you notice anything else missing. I'm going back to the station.'

'Will do,' Taylor said.

Angel went out through the front door. He was striding down the garden path purposefully to the front gate to the car, when he heard a woman called out, 'Inspector Angel. Inspector Angel.'

He stopped and looked round. It was Mrs Cowdrey, the woman from next door. She was halfway down her drive and running towards him. He waved a friendly hand and smiled. They met on the pavement by his car.

'Have you a minute, Inspector?' she said, red faced and panting. She didn't look very happy.

'Yes, of course, Mrs Cowdrey. What can I do for you?'

'Last night, Inspector. It was awful again.'

His face creased. 'Again?' he said. 'What happened *again*?'

'Have you found the snake?'

'Not yet. We will. What happened *again*?'

'Noises,' she said quickly. 'If you haven't found it, it could still be in there,' she said nodding towards Eveline Pierce's bungalow.

'It isn't,' he said. 'Our forensic team would have found it. What noises?'

'I've read that they can hide away and sleep without food for weeks at a time. It could hide under the floorboards or in the gap in the walls. I bet that that's where that snake is now.'

Angel licked his lips with the tip of his tongue, then ran his hand across his chin. 'Mrs Cowdrey,' he said slowly, 'are you going to tell me about the noises?'

She frowned briefly then said, 'Yes, well . . . last night . . . really, it was the early hours of this morning . . . I heard something, a noise. It came from next door. I can't describe it . . . it was noise . . . I was trying to get back to sleep. I tried to ignore it . . . I put it down to my imagination . . . I can't describe it but it was followed by a very short interlude . . . three or four notes at most from that music box . . . then silence.'

'You didn't see anybody?'

Her mouth opened wide. She stared at him, her eyes shining. 'Of course not. I was terrified. I was in bed trying to sleep. The last thing I wanted to do was to draw attention to myself. I snuggled down under the duvet hoping that it would all go away. But I didn't get to sleep. I got up when it was light and made my mind up to leave this place. I can't live like this. So I rang up the estate agents and put my lovely bungalow on the market. The man who does the signs has only just gone.'

'I'm sorry you feel like this, Mrs Cowdrey. But I can assure you that that snake is not there anymore, and as snakes do not play music boxes, it was a human being who returned for something and he or she won't be back.'

She frowned then said, 'What did the human being return for?'

'We are not certain,' he said, 'but I can tell you that you won't be troubled by the distant sound of that music box from there anymore.'

There were a few more questions from Mrs Cowdrey that Angel had to field before he was able to break away from her courteously, get in the car and start the engine.

As he drove the BMW on the ring road towards the station, one significant matter came to the forefront of his mind: assuming it *was* the murderer who returned to Eveline Pierce's bungalow, wasn't he (or she) taking a huge risk merely to collect a music box ostensibly worth twenty or thirty pounds? Was there something about it that made it more valuable than SOC or he could see? Was that trip back to the scene of the crime by the murderer really worth taking the risk of being seen and caught? Because if or when the murderer is caught, he or she will certainly get life imprisonment.

A flash of inspiration suddenly came to him. Wow! If the music box at Eveline Price's bungalow was worth the risk of returning to the scene for, then what are the odds that he or she might return to Elaine Lax's house to recover John Logan's music box?

He must go there immediately. He was on the ring road driving away from it.

He took the next turn left into an estate of houses, then two more left turns and then a right, brought the BMW back and travelling directly towards Elaine Lax's house.

TEN

'Good afternoon, Mrs Lax,' Angel said. 'Sorry to trouble you but there's something in Mr Logan's room I would just like to check.'

Elaine Lax peered round the door at him with small black, suspicious eyes until a look of recognition came over her. 'Oh. It's Inspector Angel, isn't it?' she said.

He smiled and removed his hat. 'Yes indeed, Mrs Lax.'

She opened the door further. 'Come in. Come in. Of course you can, Inspector. I am expecting a man from the antique dealers at half past. I thought it was him. You know the way. Nothing's been touched.'

'Thank you so much, Mrs Lax.'

'I just mashed some tea, would you like a cup?'

'No thank you. Don't bother about me.'

'It's no bother.'

She stepped back to allow him to pass in front of her, then he made his way along the hall to the bottom of the stairs. He was on the stairs when he heard the doorbell ring downstairs, followed by an exchange of convivial voices. Mrs Lax's visitor, a man from an antique dealer's she had said, must have arrived.

He continued his way along the landing to Logan's room. A flicker of apprehension hit him as he put his hand on the doorknob. He noticed his heart beating faster. He coughed to clear his throat. He turned the knob. The door opened. His eyes, like a camera, rapidly panned the room and zoomed onto Logan's desk. And there in the middle of it was the music box.

His chest heaved and he slowly exhaled. He darted across the room, snatched it up, opened the lid and the ballerina began to dance accompanied by the tinkling music. He let it play for a couple of seconds, then nodded satisfied that it was in perfect condition and closed the lid. He checked round the room, particularly the window and the windowsills. Everywhere seemed untouched and in order, so holding the music box securely in his hand, he went onto the landing and closed the door.

It was then that he heard Mrs Lax's voice calling up the stairs, 'Inspector! Inspector Angel, there's a cup of tea waiting for you.'

'Thank you, Mrs Lax,' he called. 'I'm coming.'

Then as he walked along the landing he heard a bang. It was the slamming of the front door.

When he reached the kitchen, he found Mrs Lax standing by the table and acting strangely. The fingers of one hand were spread out in a fan against her breastbone. The forefinger of the other hand was touching the corner of her mouth. She was facing the closed door like a statue.

He looked round there was nobody else there.

'What's the matter, Mrs Lax,' he said.

She shook her head. 'He's gone. I don't understand it.'

He blinked. 'Who's gone?'

'The man from the auctioneers.

'What happened?'

'I don't know. He was sat here. He seemed pleasant and eager enough to see what I had to sell. Then when I called upstairs to you, he upped and was out of here like a scalded cat.'

Angel leaped into action. 'It was because you called me by name,' he said. He pushed the music box into her hand.

'Here,' he said. 'Put that somewhere very safe. What did he look like? What was he wearing?'

'A little man in a light-coloured raincoat, no hat, big shock of black hair.'

'I'll be back.'

'And his ears stuck out,' she called after him.

Angel opened the front door and ran down the path to his car. He looked both ways to see if he could see a man answering that description. There was only a young woman pushing a child in a pushchair towards him.

'Excuse me. I am a police officer. Did a man in a light raincoat and a shock of black hair rush past you two or three minutes ago?'

'Yes. He was going that way,' she said pointing down the road.

'Thank you,' he said and he rushed back to the car.

He drove the BMW to the end of the road and reached a T junction. He turned left and went along s little way then he saw a middle-aged woman walking along carrying a bag of groceries. She said she hadn't seen anybody. He thanked her and turned the car round 180 degrees. He went along two hundred metres or so and asked again. 'Yes,' the man said, which confirmed that Angel was headed in the right direction.

Soon he reached a crossroads and there was nobody around to ask. He got out of the car and looked down each road in turn. There was no sign of him and very few pedestrians about to ask.

Angel asked every pedestrian he could. That was around eleven or twelve. Nobody had seen the man.

He quickly returned to the car and drove it three hundred metres along each of the three roads, in turn. No luck. He had considered it to be his only hope. He repeated the exact exercise. And on the very last road ahead of him he saw a small man in a light-coloured raincoat with a big shock of black hair.

Angel touched the brake pedal, pulled into the side of the road, stopped the car and got out. He walked behind him gradually speeding up, when he was six paces behind, the man must have sensed Angel's presence and he looked round. Their eyes locked on each other.

Angel's lips tightened. His nose wrinkled. 'David Doyle,' he said. 'Dublin's most undesirable export!'

Doyle's eyes flashed. He gasped and expelled his breath in small moans. 'Inspector Angel. Fancy meeting you here. The finest policeman I know. Pleased to be making your acquaintance again.'

Angel shook his head. He had heard Doyle's mixture of lies, fiction and flattery many times. 'I thought you were in Belmarsh, Doyle.'

'Came out last Friday, Inspector. And I've kept out of trouble. I'm as clean as a priest's vest.'

'What were you doing at Mrs Lax's?'

Doyle frowned, screwed up his eyes and said, 'Never heard of the poor wee soul.'

'Come on. I'll take you to see her. My car's a little way back.'

Doyle's eyes darted about glancing in different directions. Then he looked at his watch. 'Erm, I'm afraid I can't. I've an appointment with . . .erm my solicitor.'

Angel grabbed him by the arm and said, 'Well, he'll have to wait. Come on.'

Four minutes later they were in Mrs Lax's kitchen.

Doyle looked decidedly unhappy. He stood there next to Angel and facing Mrs Lax.

Angel looked at her and said, 'Mrs Lax, is this the man from the antiques dealer you had the appointment with?'

'Yes, that's the man. He said his name was Negus.'

'No, no,' the Irish man said, 'I said my name was David Doyle. It's these new teeth—' he pointed at his dentures — 'I haven't got used to them yet. If the wind's in a certain direction, it *can* sound like Negus sometimes.'

Angel shook his head. He wondered if it was really worthwhile questioning him.

Mrs Lax glared irritably at him. 'He said he represented a leading antiques dealer.'

Angel said, 'And who would that be, Doyle?'

'No, no. The beautiful lady has got it wrong, Inspector. I said I would present anything she had for sale to various leading antiques dealers and try to get the best price for her.'

Mrs Lax stared angrily at him. 'But when he arrived today, he said that he was really, only interested in music boxes.'

A bell started ringing in Angel's head.

Doyle's half-closed eyes moved rapidly hither and thither. 'That was in a list of tings, my lady,' he said. 'Did I not ask you if you had any gold, gold sovereigns, Krugerrands, old silver, gemstone jewellery or music boxes?'

'You did. But that was the *first* time we met, *not* this afternoon.'

Angel's steely blue eyes glared at the man and said, 'Doyle, who has commissioned you to buy music boxes?'

A red flush crept across the Irishman's face and eventually reached his ears, which stuck out like the doors on a taxi. They became so red that looked as if they were on fire. He ran his hand across his mouth, swallowed and said, 'I don't know what you mean, Inspector. You use such big words.'

'You know full well what I mean. Who is paying you to get the music box from Mrs Lax?'

'Nobody. Nobody at all.'

'Well what's your interest in music boxes then?'

'Oh, well I love the little tingly diddly do dah, do dah day music that they make. It's the sort of music the little people would like. That is, if they exist, which I don't for one minute think that they ever did. Do you, Inspector?'

Angel and Mrs Lax exchanged glances. She was distinctly displeased and out of patience with the little Irishman. She shrugged, stood up and went out of the room.

Angel glared at him and rubbed his chin slowly for a full 30 seconds.

Doyle tried to stare him out, but after a few seconds, he swallowed and looked away.

Angel shook his head in dismay.

Mrs Lax returned with something in a plastic bag. She handed it to Angel.

'You wanted me to look after this,' she said. 'You'd better have it now.'

He took the bag, frowned, then noticing the shape, realised that it was the music box.

'Thank you,' he said then turned back to Doyle. 'Where are you living?' he said.

'Ah well now, I'm between addresses at the moment,' Doyle said. 'I'm staying temporarily at Johnson's hotel on Wakefield Road.'

Angel knew it well. But it wasn't a hotel. Far from it. It was a hostel, and it was run by a female monster referred to as Ma Johnson.

* * *

Fifteen minutes later, an irate Angel and a very uncomfortable Doyle were in the BMW travelling along Wakefield Road. They were on their way to Ma Johnson's lodging house.

Angel had had the lying Doyle empty his pockets onto Mrs Lax's kitchen table. The only interesting items were £200 in ten-pound notes in a brown envelope and a small key with a metal tag with a figure 8 stamped on it. Doyle said the money was his life savings, and the key was to open his wardrobe at Ma Johnson's on Pink Street.

The inspector considered it worth his while to look into Doyle's locker.

Angel found the turning and pulled up outside a building that looked like a 300-year-old stone woollen mill that had been deserted.

'You lead the way,' Angel said.

'Inspector Angel, dis is not really necessary. Ma Johnson won't be pleased. And I have nothing to hide.'

'Go on. In front of me. Down this ginnel. I'll follow you.'

They went down the alley to the side entrance of the building through the double doors along a short passage and immediately were confronted by two doors. One had a sign that read "Men's Dormitory," and the other door had a sign that read: "Office Closed. Open at 6 p.m. until 10 p.m. only. Positively no exceptions."

Doyle turned back to Angel and said, 'Do you want to knock, Inspector? It will come better from you.'

Angel smiled though he didn't feel like it.

He knocked on the door. A panel slid open in the wall to the right of it and a large sexless being with a near human looking face as hard as the walls on Barlinnie prison in Glasgow, said, 'Can't you read the sign?'

Angel said, 'It's all right, Ma. It's me. Michael Angel. I'm on police business.'

'Oh yes, Michael,' she said with a sniff, 'haven't seen you lately.'

Then she noticed Doyle looking down at the floor. 'I see you've got one of mine. What do you want?'

'This man says he's staying here?' Angel said.

Doyle nodded.

'That's right,' she said. 'He's David Doyle. He's in bed eight. You'll be wanting to see his locker.'

She looked down and pressed or switched something. The sound of several bolts sliding then thudding made the door behind them shake.

'The door is unlocked,' Ma Johnson said. 'Don't be long. Let me know when you leave.'

The panel in the wall closed.

Angel tried the dormitory door. It was unlocked so he pushed it further open and gestured for Doyle to lead the way.

'I don't really have to do this, Inspector without my solicitor.'

'If you've nothing to hide, it won't matter, will it?'

'It's interfering in my private life.'

Angel's face creased. 'Let's get on with it, Doyle.'

It was a huge room with about forty beds with a grey blanket over each one and a small, plain wooden locker the size of a hat box on legs at the side of each bed. There was a number stencilled on the door of each locker. Number 8 was near the entrance, easy to find.

Doyle shuffled in and said, 'This is my bed, Inspector.'

Angel saw that the locker door was secured with a small padlock.

He passed Doyle the key.

'Unlock it, and put everything on the bed,' Angel said.

'You're going to see all my personal private things now, Inspector, and I think I should have my solicitor here now.'

Angel shook his head slowly. 'Why? What have you got in there, Doyle, a sub machine gun?'

'It's the principle I am talking about.'

Doyle opened the locker door and took out several rolled bundles of clothes in various states of cleanliness and put them in a row on the bed.

'That's de lot,' he said, then he stood with his back to the locker.

Angel unrolled each bundle and shook each piece of clothing to see what might drop out. Nothing did. He frowned. 'Is that all there is?'

'Yus,' Doyle said, shuffling back a little nearer the locker.

Angel came round from the other side of the bed, gently moved Doyle away from the open locker and looked inside it. Flat on the bottom of the locker he saw a slim official blue book. He picked it up. It was a savings book with the Northern Bank, Huddersfield Road, Bromersley.

'What's this?' Angel said as he opened it.

Doyle pouted. 'It's my life savings,' he said. 'And it has nothing to do with you.'

Angel discovered that the account it had been opened very recently. The initial deposit was £250 last Monday, and another £250 on Wednesday. Those were the days of the two murders.

'You've £500 in this account, Doyle,' Angel said. 'That's a lot of money. Where did you get all this from?'

Doyle blinked and said, 'It's all my savings, Inspector.'

'You've saved £500 in three days!'

'No. It's what I've saved over the years.'

'You had £200 in an envelope in your pocket. That's £700!'

'I had £800 in my pocket a week or two back, but you've got to spend to live, Inspector.'

The inspector couldn't argue with that.

Angel was certain that Doyle was in some way implicated in the murders, but he considered that he had insufficient evidence to charge him with anything. As long as Doyle stuck to his story, a jury would be certain to find him not guilty. Angel would like to penetrate that wall of silence but he didn't know how. He knew that he hadn't enough on him to hold him. He would have to release him, but not before he made some special arrangements.

* * *

Angel returned to the police station. He was carefully carrying the music box in a plastic bag. He had brought Doyle with him. He handed him over to the PC in charge of the cells.

'Give him a cup of tea lad, and then leave him be,' he said quietly out of Doyle's hearing.

Angel wanted Doyle to think things out for himself.

'Right, sir,' the PC said.

Angel then went along to his office. He put the music box on the table behind him. Then he leaned back in the chair deep in thought. After a few moments he reached out for the phone and spoke to Cadet Jagger.

'Cassie, will you find DS Crisp and DC Scrivens and ask them to come to my office ASAP? And then contact DS Carter and ask her to call in before she goes home?'

He replaced the phone, reached into a drawer for the telephone directory and found a number he occasionally used. It was the Probation Service.

He identified himself then asked to speak to the case officer dealing with David Doyle. He was asked when and from where he was released, and Angel was able to tell them that Doyle was released on 28 March from Belmarsh.

Eventually a young woman came on the line and said, 'I am dealing with David Doyle, Inspector. How can I help?'

'Thank you,' Angel said. 'He is assisting us with our enquiries. I may need to be able to reach him at short notice, so I would like to know whether he is committed to staying around here, and how good his attendance record is.'

'Doyle can of course move at any time, Inspector,' she said, 'but he would need to notify us beforehand. His attendance record is very good, but he never asks about a job. I've had a try at getting him employment, but it's difficult placing him. He has no trade qualifications or experience and his age are against him, and, anyway, he doesn't want to work. His attendance record is excellent, but he wouldn't receive his subsistence allowance voucher if he didn't keep his appointments. I suspect that that is his motivation.'

'Hmm, well thank you. And something else. Does he have any relation or close friend living around here?'

'We have no note of anyone. He says he hasn't any family.'

He thanked the woman, closed the phone then rubbed his chin thoughtfully.

Then there was a knock at the door.

It was DC Scrivens.

'I want you to work this weekend, Ted,' Angel said.

Scrivens' face brightened. 'That's great, sir. I can do with the overtime. I want to get married as soon as my girl, Louise and I can get the deposit on a house together.'

Angel smiled. He remembered what a struggle he and Mary had had buying their first house.

Crisp knocked on the door and came in.

'Sit down, Trevor,' Angel said. 'I want you to do some over time this weekend.'

Crisp's face dropped. 'I don't know whether I can—'

Angel was ready for him. 'Don't worry about it. If you can't, I can get Flora to do it.'

'It's just that I will have to cancel a date I had with . . . it's all right, sir. Yes. I can cancel it.'

'Right,' Angel said. 'Listen up. The situation is this.'

He then ranged over the murders of both victims, summarised the pertinent facts gathered so far, and highlighted the details of Doyle's apparent interest in the music box on John Logan's desk at Mrs Lax's, also he told them of the happenstance of Doyle acquiring £250 on each day of the murders.

'So, your mark is David Doyle, his age is thought to be about fifty or fifty-five. There is some uncertainty about that. He is such a liar. He gives a different age every time he is asked. He has served time several times petty crimes, for stealing and once for being drunk and disorderly. You should work in relays, and I'll let you work that out between yourselves. He's currently in a cell in the station. You can familiarise yourselves with him through the observation slot. Do that now. I propose to interview him again in a few minutes then I will release him. Also there are pictures of him on Records online. He is booked into Ma Johnson's tonight, so you can start outside there first thing in the morning. You're excused the CID clothes and personal presentation dress code, of course. Wear casual clothes and forget to shave. I need you to report to me twice a day on your mobiles and if anything vital happens. Any questions.'

'Is the van in use, sir?' Crisp said.

He was referring to a plain unmarked white Ford van allocated to CID for use in these sorts of situations.

'Well you mustn't use a station car. You will look too smart. I'll arrange for the van to be made available to you. Anything else?'

Crisp and Scrivens looked at each other with raised eyebrows. Neither spoke.

'Right,' Angel said. 'Leave it with you. And *keep in touch*.'

They went out, Crisp looking deadpan, and Scrivens energized but also apprehensive at the mission ahead.

Seconds later, DS Carter knocked at the door.

'Come in. Sit down, Flora. I've got a job for you,' he said. 'An extremely important job.'

He turned round to his table, picked up the plastic bag, took out the music box and placed it on the desk facing her.

'This is the actual music box that was played at the scene of the murder of John Logan. We also know that another similar box (which has since been stolen) was played at the murder of Eveline Pierce 48 hours earlier. I want you to go to the local gift shops, fancy goods shops, and find out who stocks them. Then I want you to see if the sales staff can remember who they sold them to. It would be good if they could recall anybody who recently bought more than one. It would be brilliant if you could get a description from them of such a person. That person, he or she, could be our murderer.'

Flora blinked. She knew it was a significant job, she sighed.

'Any questions,' Angel said.

'No sir,' Flora said.

Angel put the music box back in the bag and handed it to her. 'Don't lose it. It will be a court exhibit.'

'No, sir. I won't,' she said and went out.

* * *

'For the last time, Doyle,' Angel said, 'who is paying you to retrieve those music boxes and why?'

'Nobody at all, Inspector, sir,' Doyle said. 'I have said, sir, musical boxes are easy to sell and make a few pounds. Honestly, Inspector, you've got me all wrong. I wouldn't lie to you now, would I? You've known me for a few years now and since I drank the holy water at the shrine of Our Lady in Knock I am bound on oath to always speak the truth. I can do no other.'

Angel's face creased with disdain as he heard Doyle use religion to try to make himself appear to be honest, upright and respectable.

'Very well, I am going to let you go, but stay in the neighbourhood in case we have further questions for you.'

Doyle's face lit up. 'Oh tank you, Inspector, sir,' he said. 'Tank you very much, sir. Of course I will stay here. You needn't worry on that score. Oh you are a great man, a kind man. You will be blessed by all that's holy, I am sure.'

Angel cringed again. He hoped that releasing Doyle would prove to be a wise move.

ELEVEN

It was nine o'clock on that dry, windy Saturday morning when the untidy figure of David Doyle stepped out of the side door of Ma Johnson's dosshouse and shuffled down the ginnel into Pink Street, making his way onto Wakefield Road.

He didn't notice DC Edward Scrivens in his father's old overcoat and a thick woollen scarf wound round up to his chin, climb out of the white van parked at the bottom end of the street.

He followed Doyle onto Wakefield Road and the short distance into the town centre, which was busy with shoppers. He reached the head post office in town and outside the front of it was a red telephone kiosk. Doyle stopped, put his hand on the door and looked round.

Scrivens dodged behind a stone pillar and waited.

Doyle didn't seem to notice him. He went into the red box. He dialled a number, pushed some money in the slot and spoke very briefly. He came out of the kiosk and made his way along Main Street, where the major chain stores were located next to each other. At the side of one, he turned down a narrow service road that led behind the big stores and shops.

Scrivens reached the turning and peered round the corner. He pulled out his mobile, tapped in some numbers and put it to his ear. It soon connected. He gabbled down it and waited. Seconds later the white van appeared with Crisp at the wheel. He drove it straight down the service road and out the other end.

Seconds later, into the phone Crisp said, 'Ted, Doyle's scratching about in a waste bin. I'll stay this end. If he comes out here, I'll see him and I'll let you know. You stay that end.'

'Right Sarge,' Scrivens said, keeping the phone to his ear. Then he crossed the road. He would look less conspicuous than waiting at the corner, and he had an excellent view of the service road.

A minute or so later, Doyle appeared at the service road entrance. Scrivens thought that he was carrying a small piece of cardboard. He reported it to Crisp and closed the phone.

Then Doyle seemed to be walking more determinedly somewhere. It was through the town centre and onto the Joe Gormley council estate on the outskirts of Bromersley. He trudged up McGahey Hill to the top to the frontage of a row of five small, empty and dilapidated lock-up shops with To Let posters plastered across the windows. Still holding the cardboard, Doyle went round the back of them out of sight.

Scrivens told Crisp and he brought the van up to a nearby side street, where they could observe the frontage of the shops.

Scrivens went over to the van. 'Will you watch out, Sarge, while I take off my coat?'

Then he got into the back of the van and began to unravel the scarf and take off the overcoat. He intended putting on his raincoat and hat to make a change.

'I'll have a go on foot, Ted,' Scrivens said, 'when he comes back.'

Scrivens was pleased. He wasn't used to all that walking. 'Right, Sarge,' he said busily making the change of clothes.

It was no sooner said than done.

A few moments later, Doyle appeared from behind the shops no longer holding the cardboard. Now he was carrying a small box.

'He's back,' Crisp said.

Doyle peered cautiously in each direction. There was very little life about. A woman pushing a toddler in a push chair. A small car driven slowly up the street by an elderly man with white hair. Several cars and a white van parked across the road.

Doyle seemed satisfied that he was not being followed. He shuffled forward onto the pavement and across the road towards the van.

Crisp said, 'He's coming this way.' He snatched up a newspaper and pretended to be interested in it.

'Right,' Scrivens said, crouching down in the back of the van.

Doyle shuffled past hardly noticing the van.

After a suitable time, Crisp opened the door and took up the trail.

Scrivens turned the van round and waited, phone in his hand, with the engine running.

Doyle shuffled along the back streets making several turns towards the town centre again. He eventually he arrived at another service road. It led to the rear entrances to Lady Luck Shoes, Direct Discount Chemists, Bromersley Building Society and Mario's Restaurant. Doyle made his way along the short road.

Crisp reached the service road. He stopped and peered down it. Doyle had disappeared. Crisp's fists tightened. His heart began to pump harder. It would have been unwise to follow Doyle down any dead-end pathway in case Doyle returning from his mission ran into him face to face. But while he was out of sight, he could have become suspicious and done a bunk. Crisp wasn't happy about it. He dived into his pocket for his mobile and phoned Scrivens.

'He's out of my vision, Ted!' he said breathily. 'He's disappeared down the service road which has Lady Luck Shoes on the corner. It's a blind alley. It's a cul-de-sac. Can you see what he's up to?'

Scrivens was two streets away. He revved up the van, weaved in and round traffic causing several irate drivers to apply their car horns excessively in anger. He reached the service road, tore up it, in time to see the back door of Mario's restaurant close and Doyle turning away from it carrying a brown carrier bag that seemed full to the top. He was no longer carrying the little cardboard box.

Scrivens drove to the end of the alley, turned round, came out, turned left and left again and into an empty parking spot, well out of Doyle's vision. He picked up his mobile and told Crisp what he had seen.

Meanwhile from his position at the other side of the road, Crisp saw Doyle appear at the entrance to the alley and turn left onto the busy pavement. His head was higher, his steps were faster, and the brown carrier was swinging rhythmically. He was looking altogether pleased with himself. He made his way back to the outskirts of the town to the five small, empty dilapidated shops and disappeared round the back of them out of sight again.

Crisp followed him on foot, then phoned Scrivens who brought the van up to position on the side street they had occupied before. Crisp got in.

'Is there no way we can see what he's up to?' Scrivens said.

Crisp shook his head. He rubbed his chin.

Then he reached into a bag, took out a flask and two cups. He poured out some coffee and passed one of the cups to Scrivens.

Scrivens had a sip then said, 'I'll take the next leg, Sarge.'

Then he stood up, went into the back of the van and took off the raincoat. 'I'll go coatless. That should fox him,' he said with a grin. Two minutes later he returned to his seat ready to take up the trail. He took another sip of the coffee.

Crisp had been thinking. He looked at his watch. He slipped his hand in his pocket and took out his mobile. 'I'm phoning the boss.'

'Hang on, Sarge,' Scrivens said. 'He's just come out. He's coming this way.'

Crisp pushed his mobile back in his pocket, grabbed an old newspaper and pretended to read it. Scrivens looked down and covered as much of his face as he could with the coffee beaker.

* * *

Meanwhile, in downtown Bromersley, DS Flora Carter had parked her unmarked car, picked up her shopping bag containing the music box and had made her first port of call. It was a small, smart shop with a big display of expensive handbags, gloves, belts for dresses, perfumes, purses, wallets, fashion sunglasses and so on in the window.

A pretty young girl came up to her. Flora introduced herself and asked to see the manager. She went away and come back with a very stern looking woman in a tight black dress. She was topped with a shiny black coiffure which had every hair glued in place.

'I understand you're from the police?' she said. 'I am the owner of this business. My name is Miss Toomey. What can I do for you?'

Carter produced her warrant card and badge. The woman nodded, then Carter opened her bag, took out the music box and placed it on the counter. 'Miss Toomey,' she said. 'Do you sell music boxes, exactly like this one?'

The woman opened the lid saw the ballerina revolve, heard the tingling music, closed the lid and said, 'We *have* done, why?'

'Did you sell this one?'

'Probably. But there is no certain way of knowing.'

'Will you show me one, please?'

'We only had a dozen and regrettably we are sold out.'

'Oh. And who did you buy the boxes from?'

'They are imported from Italy, I think. We bought them from a firm called, Forman and Company in London.'

'Is it possible to tell me who you sold the music boxes to? In particular, can you remember selling two or more to the same person?'

'I am afraid not. We do not keep those sorts of records.'

Flora looked down, her lips pressed tight together. She sighed. 'Pity,' she said.

Miss Toomey said, 'Yes. It was a good seller. I tried to get some more but they didn't have any. They said that the line was finished and they wouldn't be able to import that actual design again. We have had several inquiries for it since we sold out. And I don't like refusing sales.'

Flora looked up. 'Can you remember anything at all about any of the people who inquired?' she said.

'I am afraid not . . . although . . . yes, a few days ago, an odd little man came in and asked for *that* particular box. He wasn't interested in any other. I remember . . .He said it was for his mother in Killarney.'

Flora Carter's ears pricked up.

'He was Irish of course,' Miss Toomey said. 'Very broad. And very scruffy. He didn't look as if he could have afforded it. But you can't always tell by looks, can you?'

Flora's heart pounded like a Salvation Army drum.

* * *

Angel was at his desk, speaking on the phone.

'Right, Flora,' he said. 'Great stuff. Get the address and phone number of that importer. See you later.' He replaced the phone.

His chest warmed with excitement at the information.

He ran the tips of his fingers across his forehead and down his temple. This new evidence was still not enough to arrest Doyle for murder or accessory to murder. But it was getting very near. It looked as if he had been employed to acquire music boxes for the man or woman with a snake and then recoup them after the murder. What sense was there in that? Where was his motive? He supposed the only motive attractive to Doyle would be money. There would be no money coming to him directly through the murder of two schoolteachers, but it was possible that the murderer might pay him for supplying the music boxes, which would explain the deposits of £250 in the building society each day of the murders. As he wrestled with the question, he thought that £250 seemed a lot of money to pay him simply to supply a music box. Was it for Doyle to supply some other service as well, such as supplying the murder weapon itself, the snake?

He rested his head in his hands.

The phone rang.

Angel looked at it. He sighed and reached out for it. It was Crisp.

'Yes, Trevor, what have you got?'

When Crisp had reported Doyle's activities so far that morning, Angel said, 'What do you think was in the box he took to Mario's?'

'I don't know, sir. I think it was something that he got from somewhere around the back of that block of lock-up shops. Seemed to me that he swopped it with Mario or somebody there, for a full carrier bag of something. Being a restaurant, my guess is that it was food.'

Angel nodded. It made sense. But it was only a guess. 'What do you suppose was in the small box?'

In the criminal world in 2016, something in a small package fingered by a crook usually meant money, or illicit drugs.

'No idea,' Crisp said.

Angel made a decision. It was time to take a look at what the little Irish man was carrying in that box.

Angel said, 'Where exactly is that block of lock-up shops where you said Doyle visited?'

* * *

Twenty minutes later, Angel made straight for the Joe Gormley estate. He drove to the top of McGahey Hill and parked the BMW at the front of the block of the five lock-up shops. He got out of the car, stood on the pavement and absorbed the run-down state of the property including the smell. It was similar to the smell of a pigsty on a hot summer's day. He noticed the big To Let posters plastered across the inside of the windows and began to write down the name, address and telephone number of the estate agent printed at the bottom of them.

It said: "Potts for Property, 24 Westgate, Bromersley. Tel. Bromersley 125740."

Another car pulled up behind the BMW.

Inside it was DS Taylor in jeans and a T shirt. He was carrying a camera.

As he got out of the car, Taylor pulled a face. 'Whatever's that smell?' he said.

Angel nodded in the direction of the shops. 'That's what we are here to find out.'

Taylor's eyebrows shot up. 'I hope it's not what I think it is. Have you tried to get inside, sir?'

'No. Apparently Doyle entered round the back. You go ahead. Take shots of the pathway and whatever there is.'

There were fish and chip papers, cardboard and lager cans on the floor of the narrow concrete passage. At the back, there were five sturdy wooden doors with five heavy duty locks.

After a lot of clicking of the camera, Taylor said, 'I've covered that, sir.'

Angel came up the passage and looked around. The path taken by Doyle was easy to spot. Angel saw the rubbish on the narrow path, and brown tree leaves and dust trapped in cobwebs across four of the five door and the door jambs. The middle door was cobweb free.

'This is the only door that's been opened in months.'

Angel bent his knees to look closely at the lock. He tried the door handle and it confirmed the door was locked.

'Looks like it's a five-lever deadlock, Don,' he said. 'Not something I can pick easily.'

Taylor nodded. 'We won't open this door without using a crowbar, sir,' he said. 'I've got one in the boot of my car.'

Angel clenched his hands briefly. He rubbed his forehead with his fingertips.

'No,' he said. 'No. Doyle was searched twice and his locker was searched. He didn't *carry* a key. It must be hidden somewhere round here.'

Angel patted his pockets and found a ballpoint pen. He reached up and ran the blunt end of the pen, applying a small amount of pressure, methodically along the layers of cement between the bricks, feeling for loose pieces. He worked the area extending around a metre each side of the door and, considering Doyle's likely reach, around six centimetres above the door. He found several places of loose cement, but there was no key behind them. He soon finished the horizontal layers and began the very short vertical layers. It was a much longer process. And again, there were a few places but no key. The last vertical layer that he tried between two bricks he found a loose piece of cement. He carefully took it out and found a piece of stiff steel wire about fifteen centimetres long overall. It was shaped almost like a letter S with one end sharpened.

Angel looked at it, bared his teeth at it and breathed deeply and noisily.

'What you got, sir?' Taylor said.

'A bit of wire,' Angel said, still gazing at it. 'What the hell is it for? Useless. This won't open a door.'

Taylor looked on, wondering why he was there. Then he lifted his camera and said, 'Hold it up, sir. I'll photograph it.'

Angel grudgingly held it up.

Taylor pressed the button. It was done.

Angel's eyebrows suddenly shot up. His mouth dropped open. He crouched down facing the bottom of the door. There was a gap underneath it of about ¾ of a centimetre. He put the sharp end of the wire under the door and holding the other end, moved it slowly and horizontally across the concrete floor from left to the right. The unpleasant smell was even stronger from under the door. He rubbed his eyes. Then suddenly, like Archimedes exclaimed as he put his leg in a tub full of water, he said, 'By Jove, I think I've got it!'

The sharpened end of the wire had snagged on something.

He felt a lightness in the chest. His heartbeat raced. He grinned as he carefully pulled the wire out from under the door. Attached to it was a piece of fabric of some kind. He continued pulling the fabric, maintaining an even tension. The fabric or rag was filthy. It looked like the sleeve of an old shirt that had been used to wipe clean oily hands. Then he saw a key fastened to the rag with a safety pin. It shone as it slid out from under the door into the sunlight. It was a key for a five-lever lock. He quickly grabbed the rag and without unfastening the safety pin, slotted the key in the lock.

The door opened easily.

Taylor's jaw dropped.

Angel smiled. He turned to Taylor and said, 'Come on, Don. Take some pics.'

'Careful, sir. We don't know what we are in for.'

They went into the musty little room and closed the door. The place smelled vile, and it wasn't only because it was damp and not ventilated.

They both pulled faces then exchanged glances.

The smell seemed to be almost as strong as a gas. It connected with their eyes as well as their noses and throats.

'Let's find the source of that awful stink,' Taylor said.

Angel held his nose.

They were in the tiny storeroom at the back of the shop. It was full of cobwebs. There was a sink with a single tap overhanging it. The only furniture was a table and a large wall cupboard which had fallen away from the wall and was on the floor with its doors open preventing it falling flat on the floor. There was nothing inside it. The floor area was littered with broken wall tiles.

Taylor pointed his camera in every direction and clicked away.

The door into the front shop was closed.

Angel opened it and the foul smell was stronger. They met piles of screwed-up paper, cardboard and silver foil dishes which had apparently held food at some time over the past year or two.

But that wasn't the main reason for the smell.

The shop window and glass in the door had been whitewashed over. The only piece of furniture in the shop was an old-fashioned chest of drawers that had long since been crudely over painted with a cream gloss. On the top of it were more dirty foil dishes, cardboard packing and paper rubbish. On the floor near it were four silver foil dishes that had a clear liquid in them.

'Is that water, sir?' Taylor said, holding up the camera and clicking away.

'Looks like it. For an animal . . . or more than one.'

Taylor's heartbeat was racing. His face was ashen. He looked round the room. 'I don't like this, sir. There might be four? Be careful. We've no protection. No gloves. Nothing.'

Angel nodded. But his chin muscles were set tight. He needed to see what was in the chest of drawers. It was the only piece of furniture to search. He walked towards it and reached out to the two white pot knobs and slowly pulled the top drawer open 5 or 6 centimetres. He gasped when he saw what seemed the entire contents on the move. The pong was unbelievable. He wrinkled his nose and promptly closed the drawer.

'Mice,' he said. 'Sixty or seventy. Could be more.'

Taylor gasped and said, '*Mice*?'

Angel opened the other two drawers and found them the same, jammed full of grey mice, some tiny pink recently born in nests made from rags. Also there was a foil dish in each drawer with many mice of all sizes standing on the contents and eating away. The bottoms of all the drawers were covered in black mouse droppings.

'Mice throughout . . . must be a few hundred . . . maybe more.'

Taylor put the camera to his eye, and clicked away at the contents of the chest.

The mice seemed undeterred by their incursion into their abode. When Taylor had finished, Angel closed the bottom drawer.

Then he noticed at his feet two mice who had come out to look round. He moved away quickly. They seemed almost to fly back under the chest out of sight.

Angel coughed. The smell was getting onto his chest.

'Let's get out of here, Don,' he said.

'I've think we've found all there is to find, sir,' Taylor said as he took a general picture from the open door.

'Let's leave things exactly as we found them. I don't want Doyle to suspect that we've uncovered his secret.'

TWELVE

It was three o'clock before Angel and Taylor left the Joe Gormley estate. Don Taylor went straight home while Angel pointed the bonnet of the BMW towards the town centre. He was returning to the police station.

The Saturday afternoon traffic was building, and as he reached the Golden Moon restaurant in the centre of town, he was slowed and then stopped by pedestrians ahead, flooding across the road at a zebra crossing. He pulled on the handbrake, lowered the window and looked at the smart frontage of Mr Rajveer's very fine eating house. A couple came out. They were holding hands and laughing. He recognised them at once. They were Gordon Glover and Helen Thickett.

Glover looked up and around as if considering the path to take when he caught Angel's eye.

Angel put up a hand to acknowledge him.

Glover hesitated, looked away, then quickly looked back with a big, forced smile on his face.

Angel pursed his lips. He was certain that Glover had been undecided whether to acknowledge his wave or not. The man was obviously displeased or embarrassed at being observed by him. Angel understood that Glover was a widower and Helen Thickett was single. There was no need to feel guilty at taking a personable young woman out for lunch in the centre of the town in daylight. Glover could take out anyone he chose. Why that hesitation?

Angel had seen it in crooks of all types from pickpockets to murderers.

Angel could see him muttering something to Helen Thickett, who looked round. She blinked several times, wiped an eye and, through ill-fitting contact lenses, eventually found Angel and smiled and waved at him.

He was acknowledging her with a smile and a wave, when a horn blared behind him. The road ahead was clear. He let in the clutch and drove away.

He arrived at the police station and was still thinking about Glover as he walked down the corridor to his office.

DS Flora Carter caught him at the door of the CID office. She accompanied him to the few steps to his office.

'I called on the rest of the fancy goods shops in town, sir,' she said. 'None of them stocked that particular music box.'

He nodded. 'Right,' he said.

They arrived at his office.

'Sit down a minute, Flora,' he said. 'I've been thinking. Only senior teachers with bags of experience could expect to get the top job at that new school, Headlands. I suppose Mitchell, the head teacher of Bromersley Modern, could have applied. Let me have his telephone number before you go.'

He then told her about his findings in the lock-up shop at the top of McGahey Hill and said, 'I expect Doyle is involved in the awful business of breeding mice for food for snakes. I would very much like to know who actually owns the snake that is being used as a murder weapon? I suppose it could only safely be kept in captivity by somebody who has premises, such as a market gardener, a farmer or a business building of some sort that has cellars or outbuildings. I don't know about which of the schoolteachers have those sorts of places. I think on Monday, Flora, when they're all at school,

I want you surreptitiously to visit each of the teachers' homes and see who has outbuildings, sheds, garages, barns, huts and the like.'

'Right, sir,' she said. 'I know that Gordon Glover, as a farmer, will have a few outbuildings, barns and suchlike.'

Angel smiled at the coincidence. He had been thinking about him and Flora had just mentioned his name.

Then she added, 'Ah, but he isn't a teacher.'

'No,' Angel said, 'so he hasn't a motive. Or at least one that we are aware of.'

He rubbed his chin. 'I need an excuse to visit him.' He thought for a moment and then smiled.

* * *

Angel pointed the BMW towards the hamlet known as Loxham, two miles along the main Wakefield Road to the Leg O' Lamb public house, where he turned left along Buttercup Lane to Lower Bottom Farm.

He saw the sign and knew he had accurately followed Glover's directions. He turned into the farmyard and noted the several barns, garages and other semi-covered, outside buildings. He also saw a pile of assorted creosoted timber, probably fencing, with a ladder at the side of it. He made a mental note of the ladder.

He stopped the car at the door and Glover came out to meet him.

Angel put on his best Saturday smile. 'Ah, Mr Glover, thank you for seeing me at such short notice,' he said.

'Come in. Come in, my dear Inspector. You're most welcome. First door on your right, take a seat, make yourself comfortable,' Glover said as he closed the front door.

Angel's eyes were everywhere although he tried to appear disinterested in his surroundings.

He made his way into the sitting room, and found a comfortable looking Windsor chair.

Glover followed him in and sat down opposite.

The room was furnished with comfortable antique furniture. The walls were almost covered with big paintings in heavy gilt frames of women with ugly faces and miserable looking men wearing wigs.

'Firstly, Mr Glover,' Angel said, 'do you know an Irishman called David Doyle?'

Glover frowned. 'Was he a building contractor?' he said. 'There was a family of Doyles in Elsecar who were builders, but that's a long time ago now. I once met a Patrick Doyle, I think his name was.'

Angel said, 'No. The man's a bit of a crook. Interested in music boxes . . . breeds mice?'

Glover's eyes flashed. He raised his head grandly, breathed in and said, 'Certainly *not*.'

Angel said, 'It's not important.'

'Never even heard of him.'

Angel realised that he shouldn't have said that Doyle was a bit of a crook. It had provoked a disturbing reaction in Glover. He must settle him down.

'I didn't suppose you had,' he said. 'But I had to ask. We have to deal with all sorts in this business.'

'Of course you do,' Glover said evenly.

His anger had subsided. Angel was pleased about that. He went on to change the subject.

'Frankly,' he said, 'I need your help, Mr Glover. We know that the murderer has to be a teacher at Bromersley Modern, and as you know all the teachers better than anybody, except perhaps the head teacher, Mr Mitchell, I would like your opinion of the character of them . . .'

Glover was in his element and spoke fluidly about each of the remaining ten members of staff individually, pointing out all the flaws he saw in their characters and praising none of them. After about twenty minutes, he said, 'And I think that's all of them.'

'Thank you very much, Mr Glover,' Angel said. 'That will be very helpful in our further search into the explanation of the two deaths.'

Angel stood up. He looked round and said, 'You keep the house in very good order, if you don't mind my saying so? You must have some help?'

'As you may very well know, Inspector, my wife and I are divorced. I live here on my own. I have a woman who comes in every day for a few hours and does everything for me.'

'And you have no other staff?'

'Not at the moment.'

As he spoke, Angel looking round noticed through the window outside, some of the barns and outhouses. He'd give anything to look round them.

'The farm will keep you busy,' Angel said. 'Are you entirely arable or do you keep animals?'

'Entirely arable. I'm quite fortunate. The soil round here is very rich.'

'I suppose you need a lot of modern machinery and experienced hands to run an arable farm in this modern age?'

'Well I don't. I have farmers on contract to do all that needs doing. They're glad of the work.'

Angel took a calculated risk of seeming intrusive and said, 'So what's in all the outbuildings?'

'I still have all the machinery, and there's the fencing stakes and barbed wire. It's surprising what clobber you need to run a farm.'

'Really?' he said. 'How interesting.'

Angel's fishing to look round Glover's outbuildings couldn't have been more obvious.

'Would you *really* be interested, Inspector?'

'Sounds fascinating,' Angel said .

'Very well, I'll show you,' Glover said. He stood up.

Angel beamed.

Then Glover looked at his watch and said, 'Oh, I can't do that now, I have to meet somebody at 4.45 and it's gone 4.30. It will have to be some other time.'

'Perhaps tomorrow,' Angel said.

'No. Tomorrow's Sunday,' Glover said. 'After Church I settle down for a quiet day. Look, Inspector, I'll phone you sometime next week. Is that all right?'

He made for the door and without giving Angel time to reply he said, 'Now I really must get ready and go. It was nice of you to call.'

Glover held out his hand.

Angel knew he had no choice but to leave.

He shook his hand.

When he heard the front door close behind him, he knew he had been out bluffed.

* * *

It was 8.28 on Monday morning when Angel entered his office at the station. He could hardly feel refreshed and rested. He'd had a very busy Saturday and a none too quiet Sunday. He went to church with Mary and then came back to mow the lawn and assault the dandelions. In the evening, they watched TV. He yawned through a film Mary wanted to see, about an A and E department in a hospital where all the patients died and all the doctors and nurses were being divorced or deserted by their respective partners. Then he dozed his way through a noisy, colourful dancing competition that had Mary on the edge of her seat.

Monday morning was back to reality. To sweeten it, there was the usual piece of cake on a plate put there by Cassie. Almost certainly from that new Paradise Bakery. It looked most tempting. He picked up the slice. It was a light as a feather. He took a big bite. It was coconut cake. He should have realised that, because it had coconut flakes on the top of it. He took another bite and it was gone. He wiped his fingers on his handkerchief. He put the handkerchief away. And it was down to business.

He reached out for the phone and tapped in a number. It was to Don Taylor of SOCO.

'Ah, Don,' he said. 'This is urgent. There's a ladder in the yard at Glover's farm. I want you to take a mould of the feet of it. Better do both ends. See if it is the one used at the murder of John Logan. And whatever the result, give me a ring on my mobile.'

'I'll see to it straightaway, sir,' Taylor said.

Angel cancelled the call then took that brown envelope out of his inside pocket and consulted the notes he had made on the back of it.

Then he tapped in a Bromersley number and was soon speaking to a Mr Potts, estate agent. He identified himself and then said, 'You have a property of five shops to let at the top of McGahey Hill on the Joe Gormley estate.'

'Yes, we have,' Potts said. 'Highly desirable property, and the rent is very reasonable.'

'I don't want to rent them. I simply need to know who owns them.'

'That's Mr Glover, the farmer. He inherited them from his father who was a big property owner in the 80s and 90s.'

'Is that Gordon Glover, Lower Bottom Farm, Loxham?'

'That's the one.'

Angel replaced the phone. He rubbed his chin. He felt that warm buzz of anticipation in his stomach. Everything was falling into place.

He consulted his notes again, then he tapped in a London telephone number. He was soon speaking to Mr Charles Forman, principal of the importers of the music boxes. Angel explained who he was and that he needed some information about a specific music box.

'Can you tell me about the availability of that box?'

'We are the sole importers of that particular model,' Foreman said. 'It was made in China and that manufacturer was producing a large range of music boxes. They sold very well and the factory was overwhelmed with orders, so they wanted to simplify the range to streamline production, that's all. They stopped making that one and several others more than a year ago. We had a few gross in stock but we sold out around last May, eleven months ago. Our customer in Bromersley was the only stockist of that particular one around South Yorkshire.'

Angel nodded knowingly. 'Thank you, Mr Forman. Goodbye.'

He slowly replaced the phone. He was thinking. The corners of his mouth turned down. That information further confirmed the deviousness of David Doyle. That man had matured into serious crime. He was no longer to be seen as the Charlie Chaplin of the criminal classes.

Angel rubbed his chin. Before he did anything else, he wanted to speak to the head teacher at Bromersley Modern, Leslie Mitchell.

* * *

Twenty minutes later, Angel entered Bromersley Modern School and was shown into Mitchell's office by a rather sulky Helen Thickett. Her lack of courtesy had no effect on Angel whatsoever.

Mitchell looked up at Angel from his correspondence, smiled and indicated the chair opposite him.

'Thank you, Mr Mitchell,' Angel said. 'I noticed that you were on first name terms with Gordon Glover and I wanted to ask you how well you knew him.'

'Well, yes. I suppose I know him as well as anybody. I knew him from when I was a junior English teacher here and he was a caring, conscientious parent.'

Angel raised his eyebrows.

Mitchell said, 'He and his wife used to attend most of the parent/teacher gatherings and showed great interest in their son's education and welfare. Their son was a difficult boy. He was backward, an unhappy introvert and given to sulking. A very difficult boy. The opposite of his father. Gordon paid for the boy to have extra Latin and geography lessons out of school hours, but it didn't really improve things.'

'What happened then?' Angel said.

'There were a few years of this. Gordon wanted his son — his name was Peter — he had wanted Peter to go to university. He would never have passed the entrance examination. Peter wasted a couple of years in the sixth form and left at about age seventeen. As soon as he left school he left home. I don't know what became of him. Shortly after that, Gordon's wife left him. He took it very badly and lived the life of a monk for a few years then, suddenly, he came out of his shell and started looking at women in a new light. Nowadays he has been seen with several women . . . all young enough to be his daughter.'

Angel nodded grimly. He thought for a few seconds then said, 'Thank you very much, Mr Mitchell. That's all I needed to know.'

* * *

He quickly returned to the station. His mobile phone in his pocket was ringing as he was rushing down the corridor. It was Don Taylor of SOCO.

'We've taken a mould of the ladder in Gordon Glover's farmyard, and compared it with the mould from the garden where John Logan was murdered on 6 April. And they match.'

Angel sighed. At last, a breakthrough. 'No doubt about it?'

'No, sir,' Taylor said. 'None.'

'Thank you, Don. Thank you very much,' Angel said slowly. His thoughts were now tightly focussed on getting the case against the murderer, Gordon Glover sewn up tight. He closed the phone. He sighed again. He felt ten years younger. He needed to find that snake. He reached the CID office and looked in. There was only Cadet Jagger there. She was staring at a computer screen updating data. When she saw Angel she stood up.

'Sit down, Cassie,' I want you to find DS Carter for me and ask her to come to my office ASAP.'

'Right, sir.'

He then went into his own office.

Flora Carter was eventually found. Angel updated her with the latest situation. She was also delighted with the news, then he told her to find a JP and get a warrant to search Gordon Glover's house and farm. She dashed off.

Then his mobile phone rang. He frowned. He reached down into his pocket, opened it up and saw that it was Mary ringing.

'Yes, love,' he said. 'Are you all right?'

'Not I'm not, Michael,' she said. 'The lights and the television keep going on and off again. It's exactly like we had before. It's driving me bats.'

'I'll have a look at it when I get home.'

'I can't wait while then. Last time this happened, Lance White fixed it in a few seconds.'

'If he can fix it, then I will surely be able to do it.'

'As a matter of fact, I've already rung the Three Horseshoes. You remember, Lance was engaged to a girl who was working there . . . Dawn something or other. Well, I've phoned there and the landlord said that neither of them were there. I don't know where he might be.'

'*Lance White*?' Angel's face muscles tightened. He wasn't pleased. 'I don't *trust* that man, Mary. You *know* he's got it in for me. Besides, well, he's not an electrician. If he can put it right in a few seconds, I should be able to. I wouldn't want to be beholden to him. We don't have to be dependent on an ex-lag to do repairs for us for handouts, Mary. I'll sort it out when I come home.'

'Oh no, Michael. I can't wait until then. I can't get on with anything. As soon as I start vacuuming, it goes off and then if I wait a bit it goes on . . . it's *driving me mad*!'

'Well go out and do some shopping. Or visit somebody. I'll try and get home early.'

'All right. I'll do what I can. I might visit Iris next door.'

She ended the call.

Angel slammed the mobile down on the desk. He gritted his teeth and ran his hand through his hair.

* * *

It was an hour later. The time was 11.45. The phone rang.

It was Sergeant Clifton in the operation room, 'Sorry to bother you. Sir, but I've just had an urgent call from West Yorkshire Police. They want us to know that they have arrested two of the gang that robbed that mill in Cubley Bottom. They blew open the safe and took a hundredweight of Zyxantium, commonly known as Looloo. They reckoned it had a street value of 4 million. They are looking for the third member of the gang who they say was Lance White. They thought he might be in our area. He was the leader and the jellyman. They say he was a whizz kid with electrics. He was educated to university level while he was serving time in Pentonville.'

'*A whizz kid with electrics*!' Angel said. '*A jellyman*?'

The hairs on the back of Angel's neck stood proud. He thought of that business with the lights and telly going on and off, his access to gelignite, his need of an alarm clock, a whizz kid in electrics . . . Angel's mind was in turmoil.

He banged down the phone, dashed out of the office, raced up the corridor to the rear exit. He must get home. He must see that Mary is safe.

He raced in the BMW through Bromersley town to the Forest Hill Estate to 30 Park Street. He left the car door open and the engine running. He ran up the path to the back door. Went inside.

Mary was busy in the kitchen. She stared at him. 'Whatever's the matter?'

'Are you all right?' he said.

Mary stared at him. 'Of course. If you've come to fix the electrics, they're OK now.'

'Is Lance White here?' Angel said.

'He called in. He must have got my message. He stopped the lights flashing. Everything's fine.'

Angel's lips eased back to show his teeth. He felt a heavy brick inside his chest. He charged out of the kitchen into the hall and opened the door into the little cubby hole where the meters are. His eyes saw four sticks of dynamite with wires sticking out leading to an alarm clock and then direct into fuse box.

His heart leaped up to his throat.

The alarm time on the clock was set to noon and the time was one minute to.

His pulse rate soared. 'It's going to go up any second,' he said, 'I want some scissors.'

He quickly switched off the mains electric supply as a precaution.

Mary arrived and said, 'What's the matter?'

'*Get me some scissors, quick*!' he yelled.

She took in the scene and gasped.

'It's going to go up, Mary!'

She dashed into the kitchen and returned with them. She slapped them into his open hand like a nurse handing a surgeon a scalpel.

He rapidly cut all the wires he could see. He took away the alarm clock. He looked at it closely, then at Mary. 'My clock,' he said. 'The one you gave to Lance White.'

The alarm clock rang while he was holding it. They both stared at it.

Mary gasped and put her arms round his neck. 'Oh Michael,' she said. 'Oh darling, if you hadn't come back . . .'

He put his arms round her and pulled her close into him.

A minute later Angel said, 'How long has he been gone?

'Oh you were right about Lance White. I feel so awful. I *am* sorry, darling.'

With a gesture of the hand he waved what she said away. 'How long has he been gone?'

'About ten minutes.'

'I want you out of here until that dynamite has been made safe. Are they in next door?'

'Iris is, yes.'

'Stay with her until the bomb squad have been. All right?'

'If you think that's best.'

'I do. Go on. Go now. As you are.'

She snatched her handbag from a chair in the kitchen and then called back, 'Be careful, darling.'

'I will, sweetheart. I will. There's nothing to worry about now. Go on. Chop chop.'

Angel half closed his eyes as he was considering the best action to take next. He turned round, closed the cubby hole door and went out to the car by the back door which he didn't lock. The car door was still open and the engine was running. He jumped in, let in the clutch and raced up to the Three Horseshoes on the corner site of Mansion Road and Rotherham Road.

It was a large public house with a large car park in the front of it. There were four cars on the car park. Angel drove the BMW onto it and parked up. He went into the pub. He picked up the name of the licensee from above the door. It was Dean Walters. The licensee recognised Angel as soon as he appeared at the bar. He was polishing glasses. There were only six customers in the place.

Angel said, 'I'm looking for Lance White.'

Walters looked skywards then pointed to a door with the word "Stairs" painted on it.

Angel crossed the room and opened the door.

He looked up the stairs then mounted them two at a time. He was almost top when White appeared at the head wearing a trench coat and carrying a suitcase.

Angel said, 'Lance White, you are under arrest for the robbery of—'

White raised the suitcase above his head and threw it directly at Angel on the stairs. He said, 'Not bloody likely!'

The suitcase hit Angel in the chest, took his breath and unsteadied his footing. He stumbled backwards but caught the handrail which he held onto with a grip of iron. The suitcase fell and bounced down the stairs behind him. It was heavy. Angel regained his balance and began to ascend the stairs. White appeared again with a bedside cabinet which he was holding up high. He threw it with force at Angel who was eight steps from the top. Angel reached for the handrail and drew back to one side. A corner of the cabinet caught him hard on the head and chest before it rolled down the stairs behind him. He quickly regained his balance and reached the landing, where White lunged at him to the chest with a hefty blow with his right fist followed through with a left to his chin, which sent Angel stumbling backwards. He fell on the floor. White took the opportunity and ran back along the corridor into a bedroom. He began to close the door when Angel arrived and threw his weight against it. There were a few hefty tries on White's part to close the door but Angel was too powerful for him and eventually White gave up. Angel pushed his way into the room. White backed off, looked round to see where he could go. He ran to the furthest corner away from the door. Angels face muscles tightened. He followed White and delivered a sharp blow with his left fist to his chin which sent him stumbling backwards, followed by another with his right and another quick jab to the left again. White fell against the wall and slid down it to the floor. Angel reached in his pocket for a pair of handcuffs and while White was dazed he handcuffed him. He then reached in his pocket for his mobile.

After he had rung the operation room for a couple of burly PCs to take White off his hands, he rang the police explosives unit at Wakefield and asked them to remove the dynamite from his house and check that everything was safe.

* * *

When Lance White had been taken off to the station by two uniformed PCs, Angel dashed back to his office to find DS Carter waiting for him with a warrant in her hand. He glanced at it then said, 'Right, Flora, thank you.'

Twenty minutes later, Angel, DS Crisp, DS Taylor and four DCs from the SOC's department arrived at the front door of Glover's farmhouse.

Angel banged the knocker and Glover appeared. He was wearing an exotic-looking silk dressing gown with a dragon down its back and he was smoking a cigar. He looked astonished at the conglomerate of police outside his door.

Angel said, 'Mr Glover, we have a warrant to search your premises.'

The man looked stunned. He took the cigar out of his mouth and stood there open-mouthed.

The police pushed past him into the house.

Glover buttonholed Angel. 'It's my wife, isn't it?' he said. 'She's put you up to this.'

Angel frowned, then he said, 'It would go in your favour, Mr Glover, if you told us where the snake or snakes are. You wouldn't want a policeman being bitten by one because you failed to warn him, would you?'

Glover looked at Angel and said, 'I don't know what you are talking about.'

'Is everything in the house and the outbuildings yours?' Angel said.

Glover's blue eyes opened wide and showing a lot of white, he said, 'Of course it is. What on earth are you looking for?'

'Do you also own those five lock-up shops at the top of McGahey Hill on the Joe Gormley estate?'

'Yes. But what the hell have they to do with anything?'

'Have you a son called Peter who used to attend Bromersley Modern, who was behind with his lessons, particularly Latin and geography?'

Glover lowered his head. He couldn't look up. After a few moments, in a small voice, he said, 'My son was backward, yes.' Then he added, 'He died of meningitis in 2008.'

THIRTEEN

It was half past four.

Angel had returned to his office and was eagerly awaiting a call from the Army Disposal Unit to say that they had removed the dynamite from his house and made everything safe. He would then contact Mary and tell her she could return to it. Also he was awaiting a call from Don Taylor, who with a team of police were still at Glover's farm. He hoped they would say that they had found a snake, or that stolen music box, or a pile of cash, or burglar's tools or the proceeds of a robbery: anything that would confirm that Glover was the murderer of the two teachers.

The silence was not promising.

Glover was in the interview room next door with his solicitor.

Taylor and his team had been rummaging round for two hours and they should be reaching the end of the search by then, even though there were several outbuildings and barns to be explored.

There was a knock at the door. 'Come in,' Angel said.

It was DS Carter. 'I've checked off the homes of the eleven remaining teachers, including the head teacher,' she said.

'Oh yes,' Angel said. 'And what have you got?'

Referring to her notebook, she said, 'All but two of them have a garage, a summerhouse, a shed, a coalhouse, an outside porch or a conservatory. The two that haven't any outbuildings are Miss Emily Parkhouse and Mr Littlejohn, the PT instructor.'

'Thank you, Flora.' He said, hoping that he would not need to know any of that.

She went out.

The phone rang. At last! Angel's stomach turned over. He snatched it up.

It was DS Taylor.

Angel's heart was banging in his chest.

'What you got, Don?'

'We've completed the search, sir, and we can't find anything to support the murder charge.'

Angel's fingers tightened round the handset. 'No snakes?' he said.

'No snakes, sir, no books on snakes, no snake food around.'

Angel ran the tip of his tongue across his bottom lip. This was not good.

'Nothing incriminating?' he said.

'Absolutely nothing, sir.'

Angel sighed. 'Right, Don,' he said. 'Stand your men down then. But bring in that ladder.'

'Got that, sir.'

Angel replaced the phone and went next door to Glover and his solicitor.

'Thank you, Mr Glover,' Angel said. 'We will not be charging you with any offence at this time. You are free to go.'

The solicitor, a bald skinny man in a smart morning suit, said, 'My client understands that all this unnecessary questioning and searching of his home was brought about by the marks of a ladder owned by him being found in the garden of one of the victims.'

Angel took an instant dislike of the man. 'The questioning and searching of Mr Glover's home *were* necessary,' he said stiffly, 'and were executed in the normal course of investigating the tragic murders of two people. The fact that the ladder was used in the execution of one of the murders was only one of several facts we uncovered. All of which have been disclosed to you.'

The solicitor sniffed. 'My client would like to make a disclosure about the ladder,' he said. 'It only came to him a few minutes ago.'

Angel blinked. Disclosures don't usually come when a suspect is being discharged. 'What's that then?'

The solicitor looked at Glover and made a gesture that he should speak.

'Yes, it's this,' Glover said. 'I loaned that ladder to Mitchell, Leslie Mitchell, the head teacher. And I've been thinking. It would be in his possession last Wednesday at the time of the murder of John Logan. He said he was painting his house.'

Angel pursed his lips. 'Thank you for that, Mr Glover. I wish you had told us that earlier. It might have made all the difference.'

He thought he heard his phone ringing in the next room.

'Excuse me,' he said and he rushed off.

He snatched up the phone. It was Captain Marriot of the Army Disposal Unit. 'Your house is safe, Inspector. We have taken possession of the dynamite, and the house and the electric supply has been thoroughly checked out. I expect you want to tell your wife that all is now OK.'

Angel sighed. 'Thank you very much.'

* * *

It was two o'clock in the early morning of Tuesday, 12 April. The sky was black as pitch and raining lions and tigers. Liverpool docks were illuminated by huge, white floodlights.

A mammoth overhead crane was transferring rope nets of mailbags from a pantechnicon on the dockside into the hold of the Royal Mail boat to Dublin.

On the quayside, standing alone in the pelting rain, hands in pockets and hat pulled down was the squidgy figure of David Doyle. He seemed to ignore the rain. He was concentrating on the loading operation, aware of the crane driver high above him in the black heavens. He couldn't see him but he knew he was there. Doyle knew that there was a moment in every transfer when the pathway of the loaded net obscured the crane driver's view of him. It was less than a second but it was long enough for his purposes. He glanced into the back of the pantechnicon. The stevedores had hooked up the last net. One of them held up his hand, rotated it and the lifting cable tightened.

This was Doyle's opportunity.

He grabbed the passing net with both hands and was whisked over the deck rail of the boat and lowered gently down into the ship's hold. The net was released and the hook disappeared upwards into the night. He then heard the humming of electric motors as the hold doors slid over his head protecting the mail from rain and thieves.

At seven o'clock the following morning, Doyle was on the quayside in Dublin. The sun was shining early. He arrived thoroughly wet and cold at the little kiosk frequented mostly by stevedores. He scoffed a bacon sandwich and slurped a mug of hot sweet tea and was soon on his way along the walkway at the side of the River Liffey.

He made his way to Heuston train station. He shuffled into the concourse. It was busy with commuters coming and going, everybody in a hurry to reach their destinations. He manoeuvred his way through them up to the train departure board. He stared up at the screen. He wanted the next train to Killarney. There was one leaving at 8.00, change at Mallow. He looked up at the station clock. It said 7.54. Just enough time to buy a platform ticket and mount the train.

* * *

It was 8.28 later that same Tuesday morning, that Angel arrived at his office. His forehead had a small cut and his temple was a bluish grey from yesterday's scrap with Lance White, but otherwise he seemed in fine fettle.

He came into the police station as usual via the back door and stopped at the cells. He looked through the observation hole in the door at the prisoner, Leslie Mitchell. He was seated on the edge of the bed looking straight ahead with an unfocussed stare.

Angel turned to the PC in charge of the cells. 'What sort of a night have you had?' he said, indicating Mitchell's cell.

'Quiet, sir. He's been no trouble. I think he slept most of the time. He's had a cup of tea. He didn't want anything to eat.'

Angel nodded and walked on to his office.

The phone was already ringing. It was Crisp.

'We're still in Liverpool, sir. We lost him after he came out of the Lancashire and Yorkshire Building Society.'

'What was he doing in there?'

'Drawing money out by the look on his face.'

Angel was thinking, he remembered that Doyle had money in the Northern Bank in Bromersley. There was no knowing how many small accounts he had. The taxman wouldn't be much interested in accounts that only amounted to a few hundred pounds, but multiply that by ten or twenty and the total amount of cash he could safely hoard away could be a tidy sum.

'Are you there, sir?' Crisp said.

'Yes, Trevor. What happened then?'

'He made his way to the docks and disappeared.'

'The docks?' Angel said. 'He might be on his way home to . . . All right, I'll take it from there. You and Scrivens come back here.'

'Right, sir.'

He ended the call, leaned back in his chair and rubbed his chin. He recalled Flora reporting that a witness in the posh gift shop said that a scruffy little Irishman, he thought to be Doyle, said that he wanted that particular music box for his mother in Killarney. Of course he could have made all that up but it might be the lead he needed.

He leaned forward and reached for the phone. He rang the Garda Síochána in Dublin.

* * *

It was twenty minutes past two. The diesel pounded into Killarney railway station. It was an hour late.

Doyle was at the carriage door with the window down. He smiled when he saw the word "Killarney" glide past him as the train pulled into the station. He shuffled off the train onto the platform with a dozen or so other travellers. At the barrier, he handed in the ticket he had dipped from a man he had contrived to bump into as they passed in the corridor as the train entered a tunnel.

He shuffled down the concourse of Killarney station, turned to the bus station adjacent and found the local bus which was to deliver him directly to his destination.

He sat in the waiting bus at its regular position and smiled. His pockets bulged with Euros and he couldn't wait to spoil his youngest boy, Sean, and the boy's mother, the love of his life, Kathleen, a buxom woman of some eighteen years his junior. She was his latest partner. His other children lived with their biological mothers except two who had reached maturity and had broken away to set up their own households with partners. He looked forward to seeing them all. He reckoned he had only a day or so before the Garda would be knocking on his door. He had only twenty-four hours to vacate his present address for one miles away. He had spent enough time in prison to know that he could never go back there again. He had to pack up there furniture and bits and bobs and move somewhere even more west than Killarney. Somewhere nice, also where there was some easy money.

It was just at that point when through the bus window, he saw a boy on the pavement pushing a barrow laden with chrysanthemums. He dashed out of the bus and soon returned with a big bunch of blooms. He looked at them proudly as he mounted the bus and shuffled down the aisle. Some of the women on the bus smiled at the little man as he reached his seat.

A driver duly arrived, took the fares, started up the engine and drove the bus out of the station. A very few minutes later it stopped at Doyle's request on Casement Road. He descended the steps of the bus tired, wet, hungry and in need of a bath. He was bursting to see young Sean and Kathleen. They weren't expecting him so it would be a great surprise.

He reached the door of number 73 in the middle of a long row of terraced houses. He turned the knob and walked in.

The first thing he saw was a man — a stranger — sat in his chair at the side of the fire, with a mug of something in his hand. Their eyes met. Doyle's lips tightened. His heart pounded. His face went scarlet.

'What's this?' Doyle said. 'What the bloody hell is going on here?'

Standing at the other side of the fireplace was Kathleen. She had been busy washing something at the sink. When she saw Doyle, her face lit up, she smiled, held out her arms to him and said, 'David, oh me darling.'

The stranger stood up. He was broad, tall and handsome.

Then she looked from Doyle to the big man and back. She realised what Doyle must be thinking. 'It's nothing like that, David, honest to God,' Kathleen said. 'He's from the Garda.'

As soon as the word Garda left her lips, Doyle's jaw dropped. He pushed the flowers into her plentiful bosom, turned and made a dash for the door.

As it happened, another big man was on the other side of it. He was just coming in. He grabbed Doyle by the back of his coat collar, pulled it upwards, dragged him back into the kitchen, closed the door with his knee and said, 'Are you David Doyle?'

Under normal circumstances, to the Garda, he would have answered in the negative, but these were far from normal circumstances.

He wrinkled his nose and said, 'Yus. What do you want?'

'The English police want to interview you urgently in connection with two murders.'

Doyle's hands shook. 'I don't know nothing about them,' he said.

Kathleen crossed the kitchen, put her arms round him and said, 'Oh David, what have you been up to?'

His lips tightened. 'I haven't been up to anything, Kathleen. It's the troot.'

The first Garda came up to him and said, 'Well, we've got a warrant and an extradition order with your name on them, so let's get on with it.'

He produced a pair of handcuffs. 'Put your hands out together, Doyle,' he said. 'Come on. You know the drill.'

* * *

That same afternoon, there was a knock on Angel's office door. It was Flora. There was a look of excitement and pleasure about her. 'I've only just heard, sir, that you've charged the Mitchell with the murders.'

'That's right,' Angel said.

'I didn't know he had a motive, sir.'

'Like many others, Flora. He wanted the headship of Headlands Community College. Eveline Pierce and John Logan were serious competition, and they were younger than he was.'

'Also that you found a pile of cash and some parcels of Zyxantium hidden in his house.'

He wrinkled his nose. 'Yes. That's the end of *that* stuff. It will be burnt under close supervision.'

'What about the snake, sir? Did you find it? Was there more than one?'

'No. Just the one. It was found in excellent condition, dormant in a bedroom in a glass tank with a hot light shining down on it.'

Her opened wide. Her jaw dropped. 'Wow!' she said.

'It will be offered to a zoo, eventually.'

She nodded. 'And what was the point of the music box, sir?'

'It was a signal to lure the snake to where its favourite food was awaiting. That's why witnesses heard the music in the night. It was from Mitchell's music box being played from outside the window.'

'And *what* was its favourite food, sir?'

Angel hesitated before saying, 'Mice.'

Flora shuddered as she thought about it. Then she said, 'What about Doyle, sir. Are you charging him with anything?'

Angel ran his fingers across his forehead. 'I am not sure,' he said. 'He supplied mice to Valerie Downing in exchange for food for them. If he read the newspapers, he would have known what she was doing with them. But that might be difficult to prove. After all, you can't prosecute a shop assistant for selling a man a bread knife which he then goes home and sticks into his wife's heart, can you?'

'He also supplied mice to Mitchell to feed his snake, sir,' Flora said.

'But that doesn't mean to say that he is necessarily committing an offence, if he didn't know what use Mitchell was making of his snake.'

'It was in all the papers, sir. Anyway, didn't he steal the music box from Eveline Pierce's dressing table for Mitchell for money?'

'He did. He did. And he tried to appropriate the music box left in John Logan's room from Mrs Lax. It really all hinges on fine points about what he knew.' Angel glanced up at the clock, 'Anyway, I am hoping the Irish Garda will have picked him up by now. I'm waiting to hear from them.'

* * *

It was 3 o'clock.

Angel was reading a longwinded police booklet mostly about Zyxantium, commonly known as Looloo. It was headed: “CONFIDENTIAL. Report on distribution of drugs throughout the UK. Dated February 2016.”

The phone rang. He looked at it. He was pleased for the relief.

He put the phone to his ear and said, ‘Angel.’

It was a PC at reception. ‘There’s a Miss Valerie Downing and a Mr Stefan Peruzzi to see you, sir. They say they have an appointment.’

Angel looked up at the clock. They were spot on time.

‘Will you escort them down to my office, Constable?’

‘Right, sir.’

When the visitors were both seated, Angel looked at them both and nodded.

Valerie Downing had a pasted-on smile and eyes that hardly blinked, while the pupils of Stefan Peruzzi’s eyes were big in a sea of white and he kept looking round the office and blinking repeatedly.

Angel said, ‘Thank you for coming in. Now I am sure that you are both very busy people, so I won’t beat about the bush. Detective Sergeant Crisp tells me that all these incidents that keep happening at Mario’s restaurant, while they are very annoying to customers and aggravating to Mr Giannini, would seem in themselves too trivial to bring to court, but the stealing of the £300 from the cash till is definitely out and out stealing, furthermore—’

Valerie Downing in a small voice said, ‘Excuse me, Inspector, but that money . . . that £300 has been paid back. It appeared as a deposit on Mario’s statement a few days ago.’

‘Oh?’ Angel said. He pursed his lips then rubbed his chin. ‘Oh. Well it doesn’t alter the case. It was still stolen. And I understand that it was impossible to have been taken by anybody other than Mario Giannini, or one of you two.’

Peruzzi jumped up and said, ‘No, sir. I woulda take er nothing from Mario Giannini. He is my besta friend. I would not take a single lira from him.’

‘Sit down, please, Mr Peruzzi,’ Angel said.

The Italian had a pained expression on his face. He sat down maintaining a constant gaze into the inspector's eyes.

Valerie Downing clenched her hands and looked downwards.

'I was saying,' Angel said, 'The £300 must have been taken by Mario Giannini, or one of you two. Now Mario wouldn't have taken it. It was *his* money. If he had wanted to stage an insurance claim or something like that, he would have stolen a lot more than £300. That leaves one of you two. Similarly, as the money was the float, the one who had the trust and responsibility of it, the cashier, that's you Miss Downing, could have — indeed would have — stolen much more than £300. So the obvious thief has to be you, Mr Peruzzi.'

The Italian jumped up again. His face was red. His eyes were bulging. 'That's a not a true. I take a nothing. I never stole in my life.'

Angel looked at Valerie Downing, she was still gazing downwards.

He turned back to the Italian and said, 'Stefan Peruzzi, I am arresting you on suspicion of stealing—'

'No. No. No. That's a not right,' Peruzzi said. 'I am innocent. I take a nothing.'

Angel said, 'You do not have to say anything—'

Valerie Downing jumped to her feet. 'All right, Inspector, I admit it. I took the money. I know that you *know* I did. I have since repaid it. Leave Stefan alone. It's me you should charge.'

Peruzzi's mouth dropped open. He stared at her. '*You* Valerie? I don't believe it.'

Angel said, 'Let's all sit down.'

When they were settled, Peruzzi looked at Valerie Downing.

'Why you do this, Valerie?' he said.

She shook her head and looked down. She sniffled and reached in her pocket for a tissue.

Angel looked at the Italian and said, 'She did it for love, Mr Peruzzi.'

Peruzzi looked up at the ceiling, raised his arms and said, 'Mama Mia! *For love*?'

Angel said, 'She also put vinegar in the cream jug, coffee in the gravy boat, innumerable mice among the cheese, and started the fire in the kitchen, didn't you, Valerie?'

She didn't look up. 'Yes,' she said in a quiet voice.

Peruzzi said, 'I donna understand. You make all this mess, do all this nuisance for *love*?'

Angel said, 'Miss Downing, would you like me to explain it to Mr Peruzzi? You can put me right if I go wrong anywhere.'

Without looking up, she nodded.

Angel rubbed his chin. 'I am not quite sure where to start, Mr Peruzzi,' he said. 'You know that Mario and his ex-wife, Dorothy, are in the throes of a divorce settlement, and Mario has to pay her half of the value of the restaurant. Well, Valerie got it into her head that if she could overnight reduce the goodwill of the business, Mario would have to pay much less. She realised that if Mario paid his ex-wife half the value of the business at its true value, it would close him down. He wouldn't be able to afford it. So she is trying to bring down the valuation figure and thus giving Mario a chance of surviving financially. Then they could get married, perhaps sell this restaurant, buy something smaller and start building it up again.'

Angel looked across at her and said, 'Is that about right, Valerie?'

She nodded.

Peruzzi said, 'So Inspector, you are not going to lock her up for that, are you?'

'I don't know. It seems to be merely crimes of nuisance, really. Nobody was actually harmed. Although cash was stolen, it has been returned. It depends upon whether Mr Giannini wants to lay charges against her.'

Peruzzi smiled. 'Oh no. He won't when he hears de troot,' he said.

FOURTEEN

It was 8.28 a.m. on Wednesday, 13 April.

Angel arrived in his office. He looked at the pile of papers on his desk and wrinkled his nose.

'Another day. Another dollar,' he said as he undid the buttons of his raincoat. He didn't know where the saying originated, but he'd heard it before somewhere.

On his desk he noticed a little plate with a thick piece of ginger coloured cake on it. It was wrapped over the plate with cling film. He smiled as thought of Cassie. He picked up the phone and tapped in a single number.

'Cadet Jagger, can I help you?'

'This looks like a giant piece of ginger cake you have left me, Cassie?'

'Yes, sir. It's genuine Geordie ginger cake, from the Paradise cake shop.'

'Well thank you very much, Cassie. And I shall enjoy it, I am sure, as I have enjoyed the other cake you have put out every day for this last week or so, but my dear wife says I am putting on weight, so please do not leave me anymore.'

'Well, all right, sir,' she said.

She was disappointed. She enjoyed going into the Paradise shop, looking at all the cakes, choosing one, slicing it, plating it up and handing it out to the team.

'It must be costing you a fortune. It's a very nice thought,' he said and he ended the call.

He looked down at the cake, peeled off the cling film and broke off a small piece from a corner. It tasted nice, and was very gingery.

He pulled the pile of pile of back post, reports, circulars, copies of "Police Review," letters and stuff in the middle of the desk close to him and began looking through it. After a few minutes, he took off his suit jacket and put it round the back of the chair. Although it was April, he allowed himself that bit of informality in the privacy of his own office. He thought it was unusually hot. In past years he had found it only necessary in the hottest months of the year, in July or August.

He kept breaking off pieces of the cake and eating it as he tackled the paperwork. Unusually, he couldn't concentrate on the matter in hand. He looked up and around the little room. He had a good feeling about being an officer in a smallish South Yorkshire police station, also, it warmed the cockles of his heart to bring to mind that he was married to a beautiful woman like Mary who seemed always ready for his advances usually in the bedroom. He smiled as he recalled that in their early days it had happened in the kitchen. It had even been known to have occurred on the stairs.

He loosened his tie. It was so hot. What was happening to that sun? He swivelled round the chair to look at the small cardboard thermometer stuck on the side of the filing cabinet with Sellotape. He treasured it. It was the only free thing he had ever had from the gas company. It said: "21°C (70F). Your ideal room temperature."

That's what it usually read.

Yet it felt distinctly warmer.

Angel removed his tie, put it on the desk and undid the top button off his shirt.

He smiled as he thought about days in the past, the warmth of the sun on his skin, the turquoise-coloured sea and the touch of the sun kissed sand slipping through his hands and between his fingers.

He remembered the first time he saw girls at school in a different light. No longer as noisy, smelly, long-haired, nuisances who for some baffling reason had to be treated like Meissen china. They became works of art wrought by God with delicious lips to be kissed, blouse buttons to be undone, and legs to be explored and caressed.

He was steaming hot. He took off his shirt and put it with the tie.

He had almost finished the ginger cake. He gathered the crumbs on the plate, bound them together to make another morsel and put it to his mouth. That was the end of the cake.

He recalled that from time to time the local press wrote pieces about him which were always complimentary. In his mind, he could see his name in headlines in the nationals, *The Times*, the *Daily Telegraph* and the *Sun*. "Angel Solves Snake Murders" or "Angel Gets His Man".

Her Majesty, the Queen sends him a letter of congratulation. The Prime Minister invites him to No 10. The BBC want to make a feature film about his life and work. There are cries in the newspapers suggesting that he is made a Lord. In his imagination he sees a door with "Lord Michael Angel" painted on it. He sees himself standing in his silk and ermine in the House of Lords at the opening of Parliament by the Queen.

He felt perspiration running from his forehead down his nose and dripping off the end. He only had a vest covering the top half of his body but he decided it had to come off. As he pulled it over his head, he realised that it was wet with perspiration. His shoes hurt. He kicked them off.

He imagined he was besieged by publishers to allow them to have his life experiences and success written up by a ghost writer and published as an autobiography. One publisher said that he might make a million or more. It sounded like a sure-fire commercial venture.

His mouth was very dry. He stood up. He was still perspiring. He felt strange and dirty. He wanted a shower and good wash. He had a feeling that he needed a thorough cleansing both outside and in. Lots of soap and cold water. He needed a purge inside. A bottle of Syrup of Figs would do it. He thought he would enjoy the relief of it all.

He went topless out of his office down the empty corridor in stocking feet to the locker room. In there was a machine that dispensed cool water. He pulled down a disposal plastic cup, filled it and drank three cups full. It tasted delicious. Cool as a mountain stream. He filled a fourth and turned away from the machine to make for the door. There was a full-length mirror fastened to the wall. He saw a reflection of himself. A senior policeman, on duty, walking about a police station half-dressed. It made him stop. He looked again. He suddenly knew that something was very wrong. It wasn't his nature. Something had happened to change him. He realised that he had been daydreaming. He didn't want to be seen like that. What would staff members think? He carefully peered up and down the corridor as he came out of the locker room and made his way carrying the water back to his office.

Once inside the office, he put the cold water down carefully. He looked around for his vest, found it, pulled it over his head, then his shirt and tie. He had to scramble on the floor for his shoes. They were under the desk somewhere.

He was not comfortable. Perspiration continued to ooze from his forehead and his neck. He went over to the window and opened it wide. He enjoyed the slight breeze. He reached out for the plastic cup of water and drank it straight off. He wondered what had happened to him. He rubbed his chin. It was the genuine Geordie ginger cake from the Paradise cake shop. He was having no more of that!

The phone rang. He looked at it. Shook his head and hoped that it was not more dreaming and that it really *was* ringing.

He reached out for it. It was his opposite number, Inspector Asquith.

'Michael, I need your help, urgently,' he said.

Angel felt befuddled and sweaty but he couldn't say no to Haydn Asquith.

'What's up?'

'Well, early this morning,' Asquith said, 'there was a triple nine, and a patrolman and the fire brigade were summoned to Darfield to respond to a report that a man had been seen in the river who appeared to be drowning. Anyway they managed to get him out of the water. It turns out he was in the altogether! In this weather! Anyway my patrolman wrapped him in a blanket and brought him in. He protested all the way here. He is in the locker room now being fitted out in denim jacket and trousers. There isn't anything else in the station he can wear. We've no underwear nor anything suitable in his size for his feet. He's still protesting. He says that he was all right and he didn't need to be rescued. I thought it was an indecent exposure case, but it isn't. Anyway, I've had a word with him. I can't make sense of him. Will you have a go?'

Angel nodded thoughtfully. With pursed lips and his eyes half closed, he said, 'Is he about six foot four, and has a lot of long brown hair and a beard?'

Asquith was surprised. 'Yeah. How did you know?'

Angel would be very interested in this character and to find out what was happening.

'I thought he would have,' Angel said. 'Of course I will, Haydn.'

'Right, Michael. I'll send him across to you.'

He replaced the phone, leaned back in the chair and gazed at the wall with unfocussed eyes as he mulled the matter over and marshalled his questions. Then he put on his jacket and straightened his tie.

It wasn't long before there was a knock at the door.

A uniformed officer said, 'The man assisting the police with inquiries, sir.' He then pushed a tall, reluctant hairy man into the room. He was clearly perspiring, particularly from the forehead.

Angel noted that the man had small piercing blue eyes and a soulful expression. He looked uncomfortable dressed in camouflaged patterned denims two sizes too small. He saw that they had found some footwear for him. He was wearing trainers.

The officer said, 'I'll be outside, sir.'

'Thank you,' Angel said and the officer closed the door.

Angel pointed to a chair and said, 'Please sit down, Mr erm . . . erm . . .'

The man didn't identify himself.

Angel had to be forthright. 'What's your name?' he said.

'It is irrelevant,' he said. 'It is forbidden for me to possess a name yet.'

Angel frowned. 'Everybody has a name. Who says it is forbidden?'

The man's face creased as if he was in pain. Eventually he said, 'The gods.'

'The gods?' Angel said. 'If you can't give me your name, how should I address you?'

'I am not clean enough to be named,' he said wringing his hands. 'I am not worthy to be on this earth. I am full of poison. I have to be cleansed. I need to be thoroughly cleansed from the inside through to the outside. Everything about me must be cleansed. The gods have told me.'

Angel blinked. He noticed that the man looked towards him and through him, but not directly at him.

'What gods?' Angel said.

'*The* gods,' he said. 'The gods that run the universe, of course. Everybody has their gods, otherwise how would you be motivated to work and reproduce?'

Angel thought that his diction and vocabulary suggested that he had been well educated.

'What do you mean?' Angel said.

'What would motivate you to get up in a morning and hunt for food?'

'What motivates you?'

'I have told you. The gods.'

Angel ran his hand hard across his mouth and jaw. 'Would you mind if I gave you a temporary name so that we can know how to address you?'

'Do as you wish. It is understood that if you do, it would not be at my request or approval. I have not yet earned a name therefore the gods would not approve.'

'Well, I will call you Rivers, after all, that's what you were pulled out of. *Mr* Rivers.'

The man pulled an unhappy face and shrugged. 'It's as bad a name as any other.'

'Where do you live?' Angel said.

'I live wherever I am at the time.'

Angel rubbed his chin and pulled a face. 'How long have you been on drugs?'

'I have never been on drugs.'

Angel rubbed his chin. 'How long have you been . . . erm like this . . . dependant on the gods?'

'From the time I was graciously given a memory.'

With his mouth open, Rivers stared thoughtfully ahead for a few seconds at nothing in particular, then he said, 'After feeling very hot, discarding my trunks and going for a swim in the river, the gods came, and they were not pleased with me.'

He suddenly stopped talking. Then he glanced round the room.

'It's very hot in here,' he said.

Angel frowned. He swivelled round the chair to look at the small cardboard thermometer. It was the same. He didn't think that that was too hot. It was only barely warm enough.

While Angel was turned away, Rivers looked down at his denims. Then he began to undo the buttons down the front of the jacket. 'I'm still very hot,' he said, 'and I am still full of poison.'

'Don't do that, Mr Rivers. We have quite a contingent of female officers in the station. We don't want to embarrass them, do we?'

Rivers stopped undoing the buttons. 'I don't want to offend *anybody*, but I can't stand this heat much longer. I need to return to the river. It is cooling in the water and I can get some more food of the gods before it is all gone.'

Angel knew his questions were achieving nothing. 'What is the food of the gods?' he asked.

'The gods, who were aware of my need despatched a chariot driven by an angel in disguise from the heavens to the woods where I live and delivered a pile of cakes from Paradise.'

Angel peered at him closely. Bells were beginning to ring. 'How do you know they were sent from the gods? Maybe somebody just dumped them?'

Rivers face suddenly brightened. 'That's the point,' Rivers said, emphasising by waving a finger. 'Of *course* somebody had dumped them. The angel had dumped them in the place I frequented regularly so that I was sure to find them. Furthermore, they were disguised in wrappers suggesting they were simply ginger cakes. But on the wrappers in and among lots of other irrelevances were the words Paradise Bakery, so I knew where they had been created and that they were specifically intended for me.'

Angel smiled. Bells were ringing. Pennies were dropping.

'I suppose they were in wrappers that said, "Genuine Geordie ginger cakes. Made in the Paradise Bakery."?'

Rivers, his head on one side, mouth open and frowning slightly looked at Angel uncertainly.

'Well, Mr Rivers,' Angel said, 'thank you very much. You've been a great help.'

He then stood up, walked to the door and opened it.

The constable was standing there with his back to the door. He turned to face him.

'The gentleman and I have finished our conversation, constable,' Angel said. 'Will you escort him back to Inspector Asquith?'

'Yes, sir.'

The man Angel had only just christened Rivers stood up and went out to join the constable. Angel closed the door, returned to his desk and picked up the phone. He tapped in a single digit.

'Haydn? That man you sent me, I think he is drugged. He's as high as a kite. I couldn't find out his name. I suggest you push him onto the duty psychiatrist who I think today is Dr Salomon.'

'Thank you, Michael. I agree with you.'

Angel cancelled the call and made another. It was to DS Carter on her mobile. 'Come up here, Flora,' he said. 'It's urgent.'

She was in CID. She only had to cross the corridor.

When she was settled, Angel said, 'It's become obvious that Cassie's favourite shop, the Paradise cake shop, is the drug distribution centre. I think that that stolen bread van was attempting to make a delivery last Friday morning when it was briefly spotted on Church Street by one of our patrolmen. I think that some of that stolen drug, Looloo, was in that ginger cake she brought. It has affected me slightly.'

Carter's eyebrows went up and she said, 'Oh? And how did it affect you, sir?'

Angel wrinkled his nose and said, 'Well, we won't go into that just now, Flora. I take it you didn't have *any*?'

'No. Keeping an eye on my weight, sir.'

'Hmmm. Well, we've got to raid that place, and we need a warrant, to search the place for illegal drugs and to arrest, as suspects, everybody on the premises. Will you write it out and get it signed? Mrs Justice Marriot is the nearest JP and she's usually at home at this time?'

'Right, sir,' she said and she dashed off.

He picked up the phone and tapped in a number. It was to DS Crisp.

'This an emergency. We are going out on a raid. Come up to my office, ASAP.'

Crisp thought raids were the most exciting part of police work and he looked forward to them. 'Right, sir,' he said. 'On my way.'

Angel ended the call and was considering how many uniformed men he should ask from Haydn Asquith. He needed to cover all the entrances, exits to the premises and to take into custody, staff and customers in the shop, in the bakery and up the stairs. He decided that ideally he would like around twelve uniformed men and that CID would provide four including himself, making sixteen in all. That should be enough.

He was about to reach out for the phone, when there was a knock at the door.

Angel glanced up. 'Come in,' he called.

It was DS Crisp. 'You wanted me, sir,' he said brightly. 'Who are we raiding?'

Angel looked up again. He was astonished at what he saw. His mouth dropped open. For a few seconds he could not speak.

Crisp was in front of him wearing only his vest, underpants, shoes and socks.

Eventually Angel said, 'What's happened, lad? Where are your clothes?'

Crisp looked down his front at his vest, bare knees and legs. Then he looked at Angel with a frown. 'I felt very hot, sir. I don't understand.'

Angel said, 'Well, where are your clothes?'

'In the CID office.'

Angel snatched up the phone and tapped in a number.

He looked up again at Crisp. 'Ooooh. Somebody might come in,' Angel said. 'Go and stand behind the end of the stationery cupboard, lad. At least you'd be partly hidden if anybody does come in.'

A voice through the earpiece said, 'CID, DC Scrivens. Can I help you?'

'This is DI Angel, Ted. Erm . . . erm . . . Are you in the CID room, lad?'

'Yes, sir,' Scrivens said.

'Good. I understand that DS Crisp has left some clothes in there.'

'Yes sir. They're on his desk. I can see them.'

'Ah, good. Bring them across into my office straightaway.'

'Right, sir.'

Angel replaced the phone. Stood up, dashed across to the stationery cupboard and opened both of its doors.

Then he looked at Crisp and said, 'Stand behind that door and keep out of sight.'

There was a knock at the door.

'Come in,' Angel called.

The door opened and Scrivens came in.

Angel looked up.

The DC was carrying a bundle of clothes but behind them, his neck, shoulders, legs and feet were bare.

Angel sucked in a quick breath. His heart seemed to freeze momentarily and then pound away.

Crisp popped his head out from behind the stationery cupboard door to see what was happening.

Scrivens saw him and smiled. 'There you are Sarge,' he said and walked towards him with the clothes.

Angel then saw the back view of the young detective.

Scrivens was as bare as the day he was born.

Angel tried to speak but his voice had gone.

THE END

ALSO BY ROGER SILVERWOOD

YORKSHIRE MURDER MYSTERIES

Book 1: THE MISSING NURSE
Book 2: THE MISSING WIFE
Book 3: THE MAN IN THE PINK SUIT
Book 4: THE MORALS OF A MURDERER
Book 5: THE AUCTION MURDERS
Book 6: THE MISSING KILLER
Book 7: THE UMBRELLA MURDERS
Book 8: THE MISSING MILLIONAIRE
Book 9: THE MISSING THIEF
Book 10: FIND THE LADY
Book 11: THE MISSING MODEL
Book 12: MURDER IN BARE FEET
Book 13: THE MISSING HUSBAND
Book 14: THE CUCKOO CLOCK MURDERS
Book 15: SHRINE TO MURDER
Book 16: THE SNUFFBOX MURDERS
Book 17: THE DOG COLLAR MURDERS
Book 18: THE CHESHIRE CAT MURDERS
Book 19: THE DIAMOND ROSARY MURDERS
Book 20: THIRTEEN STEPS TO MURDER
Book 21: THE FRUIT GUM MURDERS
Book 22: THE MONEY TREE MURDERS
Book 23: ANGEL AND THE ACTRESS
Book 24: THE MURDER LIST
Book 25: THE LIPSTICK MURDERS
Book 26: THE MUSIC BOX MURDERS

Printed in Great Britain
by Amazon

60633738R00106